About the Author

Sydney Wray is one of the most celebrated authors of her generation Z. At the age of twelve, she wrote her first novel, *The Run*, which brought 3.4 million readers and launched her career. With millions of readers and followers alike on Wattpad, an online reading and writing platform, Sydney has already positively impacted the extensive pool of YA readers. *Find a Penny, Pick Her Up* is her fifth book, winning the Watty Award for one of the best young adult fiction novels of 2022. She is now a 2023 Sewanee College graduate with an English degree and certification in creative writing.

Find a Penny, Pick Her Up

Sydney Wray

Find a Penny, Pick Her Up

Olympia Publishers
London

www.olympiapublishers.com
OLYMPIA PAPERBACK EDITION

Copyright © Sydney Wray 2024

The right of Sydney Wray to be identified as author of this work has been asserted in accordance with sections 77 and 78 of the Copyright, Designs and Patents Act 1988.

All Rights Reserved

No reproduction, copy or transmission of this publication may be made without written permission. No paragraph of this publication may be reproduced, copied or transmitted save with the written permission of the publisher, or in accordance with the provisions of the Copyright Act 1956 (as amended).

Any person who commits any unauthorized act in relation to this publication may be liable to criminal prosecution and civil claims for damage.

A CIP catalogue record for this title is available from the British Library.

ISBN: 978-1-83543-044-6

This is a work of fiction. Names, characters, places and incidents originate from the writer's imagination. Any resemblance to actual persons, living or dead, is purely coincidental.

First Published in 2024

Olympia Publishers
Tallis House
2 Tallis Street
London
EC4Y 0AB

Printed in Great Britain

Dedication

To Daydup, for being the best big sister and built-in best friend. You are the Jess to my Penny.

Acknowledgments

I'd like to share the enormous amount of transformation this story has undergone to be where it is right now, in your hands, and offer my most sincerest gratitude for the tutorage I've received that's helped mold Penny into the character she's become. I hope you love her as much as I do, and though I deeply admire all my characters and their stories, this one has forever gripped a piece of my heart.

To the professors I've encountered during my time at college… and especially for the Sewanee English department I've had the privilege of learning from. The excellence in teaching is quite unparalleled. To Professor Maha Jafri: thank you for teaching me how to view the world through a different lens. Oh, how I wish I could sit through your classes once more! Your brilliance and passion have permanently altered the way I think and write. I will always remember the squirrel's heartbeat.

Thank you to everyone on my Olympia team who had a helping hand in getting this book to your hands. A special thank you to James Houghton and the cover team who captured the magic of this story. Thank you to Imogen Arthur for your hard work!

Thank you to Kirby, Tracy Lyn, and Veronica Peterson. I'm in awe of the combined talent and kindness, thank you for your helping hand in bringing this book to its first ever print. You're awesome.

To the Wattcon judges, who captured the sparkle in this story and blessed me with an award. Thank you.

Wattpad readers! You are my one true, literary love. You saw this book first, and I thank you for sticking with Penny. Mwah!

My sister. I thank you for the (read: boring) coffee dates, Chai lattes, Nitro cold brews, and endless patience during my editing process.

My mom: you are my biggest supporter and best friend. I'm glad you're mine.

Of course, I'd like to thank the amazing Craig Bouchard, whose continuous friendship and mentorship have taught me that writing is a beautiful and wonderful thing. Years ago, during one of our many coffee meetings discussing the logistics of a business, you gave me a piece of advice: you have to be happy in order to write, and it doesn't work if you're not. Thank you for not only everything you've given me so far, but also this. For everyone who has believed in me; you do not go unnoticed.

And last, but certainly not least, you: the reader. None of this would be possible without you. Thank you, thank you, thank you. With that being said, I'm more than excited to continue this journey with you. See you soon!

Chapter 1

The heads of every—and I mean *every*—girl turned toward the stranger stepping through Royal High's front door. Held open by Mrs. Prickett, the witch grinned her perfect principal smile. She held out a beckoning arm, her tightly pressed maroon business jacket protesting from the movement. Perfection was the theme of everything she preached, though our small-town high school of four hundred and two would protest. Despite the five-star reviews from the visiting summer families, I assure you that the town of Port Royal was far from perfection. I was sure that the people who lived here for the entirety of my own seventeen years would agree with my assessment. Or maybe I'm just bitter.

I peered at the surrounding girls; every matter of their brain cells focused on the boy. I was blessed with the ability to give every attention-seeking girl their life story, favorite color, and alcoholic drink of choice. Rolling my eyes, I wished I hadn't been given such a fantastic memory. That I could forget everything and anyone involved in the accident. My tummy rolled at the thought. I would have no problem ducking my head for the rest of my high school career and moving every related detail to the trash bin. If it weren't for Jess, my last remaining friend, I would've done it already. The hallway fell almost silent, interrupted only by giggles and whispery comments.

The silence and accompanying stares of the gaping girls made me squirm. I shook my head, turning to Jess. "This is embarrassing," I said, glancing again down the line of girls, who, in all their glory, reeked of desperation.

The bright yellow lockers decorated the scene to make it picture-perfect, all ready for a *Sears* Back-to-School catalog. "What if he turns and sees?"

As if on cue, I was proven wrong. His broad shoulders turned slightly toward his audience of mesmerized girls, but not completely. The only thing to judge would be his dark wash jeans, white long sleeve pullover, and slow walk. He took off his sunglasses, his naked eyes revealed to the lucky girls closest to him. I watched a scene that resembled the most gruesomest of car wrecks; my classmates kept their shit together until he entered the main office. An eruption of giggles sounded in the hallway.

"Shh," Jess said, adding herself to the mass of girls who had just forgotten their names. Which, okay, I understood their curiosity. What kind of kid comes two months late after the start of a new school year? It was nearly November. Besides, he would soon realize that every girl was officially deprived of new boys, new conversation, and perhaps a chance to remake themselves for someone who didn't witness their first neighborhood bike ride.

The bell sounded, signaling a countdown of five minutes to period one. I turned to my locker, expecting a similar reaction from the crowd. But the clanging of metal lockers and the babble of gossip didn't erupt like it usually did. Why was everyone so invested? We all knew he'd go for Annie Prickett, as in, yes, the principal's daughter.

People are too predictable these days. I eyed myself in my locker mirror, my mascara-coated brown eyes reminding me, *Like what you used to be? Don't be a hypocrite, Penelope.* I tugged at a piece of my blonde hair, an anxious habit I'd developed following my previous reign of being a mean girl.

Jess's sigh fell in sync with everyone else. She turned to me, her dark blue eyes enlarged for effect. She played with the tail of her dark side-braid. "I bet his name is Will. William, if we're being technical."

I couldn't help but smile, slipping books into my bag and shutting the locker. "You got that by looking at him?"

She nodded her head. "I have a gift. Remember that time in eighth grade? When I guessed the kid's name, who visited for the day?"

I walked down the hallway, the sea of students veering around me like second nature. *Classic.* To them, I didn't exist any more, not since Jack. "That was such luck. And a coincidence."

Jess rolled her eyes just as we passed the office, where our mystery visitor disappeared into. "What's your guess?" I shrugged, turning a corner and spotting our classroom up ahead. She was quiet, which was out of character. My indifference bothered her more than she let on, I could tell. She wanted me to jump down the rabbit hole of the mystery man. Be a normal teenager. A normal teenage-girl who obsessed over cute—okay, one very cute boy. But neither of us had seen that side of me for a few months now. I waited for the list of excuses she'd soon offer up for why I was the way I was, ignoring the Jack-sized elephant in the room. She glanced at me in my peripheral vision. "It's not about—"

"No," I said. None of it was about Justin. He was a great part of my life; before, that is. But now? *He didn't sign up for what I did.* We reluctantly walked into the classroom.

"Okay," she said lightly. "Has he tried talking to you lately?" We sat in our usual spots, not too close to the front and not too close to the back.

"You already know the answer to that."

"Penny." She reached out and squeezed my forearm. "He just wants to be there for you."

"Can we not get into this?" I asked quietly, avoiding her concerned gaze. Just then, Mr. Hatcher entered the room and relieved me of the topic. I tried to concentrate on his opening words, his ancient voice, and his shaky tone. Jess's piercing gaze was still there. I dropped my eyes on my paper, deciding it was a good time to focus on my favorite hobby in school. Maybe I should call it therapy. I carefully drew a heart, eyeing the shakiness of my hand.

*

There was a buzz of new activity in the lunchroom. Of course, there was always some drama over who kissed who, who wanted to kiss who, and who skipped that step and went right to the finish line. But today felt different, and it didn't take an idiot to figure out why.

I glanced around the room from my position in the lunch line, taking in the infamous coordinate plane. The Southside kids were in their normal spot. We called them the PB&J's. PB's for short. They were kids who weren't likely to ever leave Port Royal; they served as spokespeople for this tiny town. If anyone wanted to stay here for the rest of their lives, he or she was probably one of the PBs. Their lives were scripted and planned. We never hung out with them. I swallowed, guilty of the thought that in another lifetime, I was a PB before Annie made me a Westsider.

My eyes cut to the entrance, a sickly familiar blonde was entering. Annie and the rest of the Mets crossed the room to the left side. It was my former crowd. Just like everyone else, my gaze followed Annie, secretly wishing I could still walk with them.

They reached the Westside, where everyone wanted to sit.

The name came from an alumni whose last name was Met. Somehow, it stuck. A sheet of glass composed the entire wall—the Westwall. It was one of Royal High's biggest attractions; whenever there were tours, Principle Prickett would bring them to see the glass wall. It was as transparent as the students, tricking the outside world into thinking there was nothing but beauty and perfection behind them, but in reality, it proved to be entirely false once piercing the surface by just a few inches.

"Can you, like, move?"

Raising an eyebrow, I peeked behind me. It was Anna. My look used to be threatening, but not any more. Anna gazed at me, starting with my head and descending to my toes, not bothering to hide her pathetic attempt in making me feel small.

She was the newest addition to the Mets—my replacement and an itty, bitty sophomore (I wasn't usually one to claim seniority, but consider me a changed woman). She was once an Eastsider, a nobody who didn't conform with Royal High's lunchroom coordinates.

Almost immediately following the accident, it was made quite clear that my steady membership as a Met was over, as was my position at the Westside table. So, Anna took my empty spot, and I hers. I'd realized that my new Eastside home had a much worse rep than it deserved; I had all the room in the world to stretch my arms, give my backpack its very own seat, and give my lunch a proper spread over the table.

Better than knocking elbows and inhaling boatloads of Gucci perfume.

Jess stood by my side during the banishment, which, by association, awarded her a one-way ticket to the Eastside. We'd staked our newly permanent positions, but I'd be lying if I said I didn't miss the feeling of being on top.

"Sorry." I stepped into the huge gap in the line I'd allowed through my day dreaming. I watched the guys take heaping portions in front of me. I grimaced, looking back at the Mets. Annie threw her head back in a loud laugh, looking perfect and having the attention of nearly every guy. I wondered which one she was trying to hook up with for that month.

Through the windows revealed the backside of the school. Cars whizzed by on a road, winding through a maze of palm trees adorned in Spanish moss. Sunlight filtered through the windows, illuminating every Met.

"I know what you're doing."

Jess suddenly appeared. She eyed Anna, noting the audience and being careful with her words.

I smiled, stepping forward in line to make room for her. "You can't cut," Anna said. "Annie said you were like that."

Jess spun around. Anna picked the wrong girl to mess with. Sure, we were both booted from the Westside. But it didn't mean that Jess had lost her fire. "Excuse me?" her tone changed.

I stared ahead, the encounter making me feel nostalgic. But in a bad way. I hadn't witnessed something like this since that night, when I was at the top of Royal High's food chain. Anna didn't respond, presumably because Jess could be scary and was a former Met. A veteran. She was there long before me. Jess turned back around, now standing beside me. I shook my head with a smile, grabbing a tray.

We passed the west and south sides, making our way to the Eastside. The Northside was usually a wasteland reserved for faculty. If a student sat there, they were nonexistent. At the *least*, I had Jess and wasn't forced to sit with Ms. May, who ate egg salad croissants and actually *liked* them. How gross was that?

We pulled out the plastic chairs and sat. There weren't many people in the east, which is why it was perfect. For me, at least. I glanced at Jess, knowing she'd rather be by the glass. Adding to my pile of guilt, I'd always feel bad for tearing Jess away from the Westside.

"Guys." Andrea bounced over to the table, her freshman frame of one hundred pounds grabbing the seat next to Jess. She was what I called a floater; she bounced back and forth between the PBs and Eastsiders.

I bit into a baby carrot. "What?"

"What's the new guy's name?"

My attention returned to the baby carrots. "I haven't heard anything," Jess said. "The Mets probably know."

"Can you ask them for me?" Andrea asked. "Because we made this bet in class that anyone who found out would get first dibs on him, and I saw him this morning, and he looked really cute, and you guys know that Jay didn't work out."

"Hey." Jess put a hand to her shoulder, silencing her. "Too much."

"Andrea…" I paused. "He's a senior. He'll probably be snatched up by another senior."

Andrea huffed. "I can at least *think* about it."

Jess changed the topic. "You're asking the wrong girls. We don't know his name."

I shrugged. "I haven't seen him since this morning." He probably took one look at the yellow lockers and got the hell out as soon as he could. If only I could.

"A girl in my class saw him walk into the bathroom after

third period," Andrea said, proud of herself.

"Did she tell you that herself?" Jess asked, her tone skeptical. I took a sip of water and leaned back.

Andrea tapped her fingers on the table. "Well, no. She told Ashley, who told Sarah, who told our English class." Jess and I met eyes, sharing a laugh. Rule one of Royal High: never believe the Rumor-Mill.

"Well, if either of you find out, will you tell me?"

"Sure." I shrugged.

"Awesome. Love you." She bounced back up, retreating to the freshman PB's. "If I'm being honest"—Jess paused, taking a bite of her grilled cheese—"I kinda want to know his name. Just to be ahead of it all."

"Annie probably already knows."

"Maybe," she said. "But you know her. Acting like she has her shit together when she really doesn't."

"Don't we all?" I asked, startling myself. Did I just stick up for Annie Prickett?

Was I still that conditioned?

Jess looked at me, probably wondering my own question. "Maybe before." Before that night, three months ago.

Chapter 2

Before ~ 11 July ~ A Time Before Drink 1

"I'm gonna go look for Justin," I said, stepping up into Eric's house. The end-of-year party—though mid-summer, Eric insisted every summer party be entitled this way to ensure its "maximum partying potential"—sounded in full swing, but Annie promised us all that it wasn't a party until we got there.

"Woah, slow down," Annie said by my side, accepting a drink from Eric himself. He grinned at Annie, like everyone else, and shut the door behind us. "We just got here."

I looked around. "I told him I'd find him once I got here."

"At least take a shot with me first." She pulled me toward the kitchen. "Be the Party-Penny we all know you are."

I laughed, letting her lead me. I had to lean into her ear so she could hear me over the music. "Party-Penny is not making an appearance tonight." Party-Penny was a household name by that point; Annie gave me my first drink freshman year, and the rest was history. The two of us entered the wide kitchen, the wooden floors gleaming and matching the cabinets. Students I recognized milled about, but my friends were already gathered around the selection of alcohol.

Annie grabbed a bottle of cheap vodka and a carton of orange juice, handing them both to me. "We'll see about that." I took them from her with a sigh. One or two pulls wouldn't hurt, right? Jess, my second favorite, and the rest of our band of five members squealed our names. We gave quick embraces, obscured by thumping music and exclamatory, "I'm so glad you're here!" and "You totally missed Tracy spilling her drink ALL over her white shirt!"

I noticed a bunch of boys gathering in a room around the corner. They yelled something that resembled a frat battle cry. I felt Annie grab my chin with her fingers, bringing it to her.

"Drink up." She smiled her dazzling smile, and it was moments like these that I wanted to be her Number One Fan. And remain it. Like she was mine.

The losers of Royal High typically tip-toed around Annie, though I didn't know why. She was nice—enough, anyway. Put yourself in my shoes: who wouldn't want to be best friends with the coolest girl in high school? Some would say she was the bitchiest girl in school, but honestly, I felt more on top than I'd ever really felt in our friendship.

We'd known each other since we were practically toddlers, and she always had a bit of a sting to her. I always felt a little lower in status compared to her, like she had this aura of being better than anyone lucky enough to stand around her. I felt it; my parents felt it.

I wasn't pretty enough in middle school to hang out with Annie Prickett, so we didn't really cross paths. But once ninth-grade hit, something shifted. She started talking to me more. Inviting me to go shopping at the mall or go people-watching at Creamy & Creamier Creamery and watch the weirdos pass by. Maybe it was because I'd traded my thin, wiry, insurance-covered glasses for contact lenses. Or maybe it was because I started highlighting my hair and using makeup. Regardless, I was given an invitation to elevate my status. How could I turn that down? Being in Annie's world was different than just walking with her to class or into parties together. It was living through her. So, I eyed the vodka in my hand, the room of gathered boys, and Annie's cocked eyebrow, waiting for me to prove to her that she'd made the right decision by befriending me.

"Oh, come on." Annie rolled her eyes, sipping her drink. "Remember what we talked about?" I did. Before we left for the party, Annie told me that a freshman had mistaken me for Annie. I made a face, though I was secretly pleased. Who knew that *I*, Penny Brooks, would be mistaken for the perfection that was Annie Prickett?

She'd laughed, shrugging. "You're my best prodigé." A smile found my face, but hers disappeared. "You better continue acting like it."

I gripped the bottle. The plastic touched my lips, burning them instantly as the liquor slid down my throat.

Chapter 3

I slammed into someone wearing perfume that smelled of aged flowers. I gasped, looking up at Mrs. Prickett. I'd developed a pattern of watching my feet, especially when I was on my way out of Royal High and into a safer environment.

"Penelope! Are you okay?" *Like she cared. Give this woman an Oscar.* I mumbled an apology, just then realizing who was standing next to Prickett. A pretty woman, a petite brunet, who looked about my mother's age, and her son, the newest celebrity of Royal High. Out of all his fangirls, why did I have to be the one who ran into him?

Literally, I might add.

"Penelope," Mrs. Prickett spoke. I bit my tongue at her use of my full first name.

This woman watched me grow up with Annie. Or at least around her. Were the class birthday parties, trunk-or-treating, and school dances not enough? And she still couldn't call me Penny? "I'd like you to meet our newest student, Hampton Prescott, and his mom. Hampton's a senior, too." Hampton looked me in the eye but said nothing.

He shared half his mother's hair color, merged with honey blonde tones that packaged a true dirty blonde. He had the same greenish hazel eyes but a narrow jaw that they did not share. "Please make him feel welcome." Mrs. Prickett directed her fake smile at Hampton.

"I'm sure Penelope will introduce you to all her friends." I looked away from Hampton toward her, knowing she knew of my current social status. I would've been the perfect person to befriend a year ago, but now it seemed useless. He belonged with someone like Annie. Besides, it was only a matter of time before she'd swoop in to make her kill.

He held out his hand, offering me a warm smile that matched his mother's. I placed my hand in his. It was soft. "It's nice to meet you." I looked at Mrs. Prickett, waiting for her to give me the go-ahead. But judging by the strain on her face, I could practically read her mind: *Gosh, I can't excuse Penelope now because it would make us look unfriendly. But I don't think Hampton's mother would appreciate me pushing the town's problem child on her son. He needs someone like Annie. But maybe if I push this more, my sweet, perfect angel of a daughter will steal him regardless. Bingo.*

Okay, maybe it wasn't exactly like that. But I'm sure I was pretty damn close because the next thing that came out of her mouth was, "Hampton, would you like Penelope to be your shadow buddy for tomorrow?" Cast me further into social suicide, why don't you?

My jaw tightened. I was the last person he needed as his buddy. Was Prickett messing with me? I looked at Hampton and said, "I don't know if that's a good idea."

My principal ignored me. "Penelope grew up in Port Royal," she said, putting a hand on my shoulder. I tried not to stiffen, remembering the last time she put a hand on me. When she watched her daughter and I leave the safety of their cookie-cutter home for a party that would be talked about for years to come.

"Hampton is from New York," Mrs. Prickett continued, like it was something we could bond over. She knew the only place I'd ever been outside of Port Royal was Georgia, when we visited the Atlanta aquarium, but I was too young then to really remember it.

"Very cool." I eyed the double doors in the distance; maybe I could escape. The bell for last period would be ringing soon, and I'd specifically arranged my schedule so I wouldn't be caught in the sea of my peers.

His eyes were locked on me. I looked away. "I should get home. Mom's making dinner." I wanted to hit myself because who makes dinner at 1.12 in the afternoon? "Welcome to Port Royal." I stepped around them and in the direction of the parking lot. Since her daughter had royally screwed my life, avoiding Mrs. Prickett had become an art form of mine. I stepped into the sunshine, wanting nothing but to get home and into my room as soon as possible. The day brought with it too many surprises. Just thinking of my silent, dark bedroom and non-judgmental bed made me ache for it.

I adjusted my backpack, annoyed. Our perfect principal could fu—

"Hey!" an unfamiliar voice interrupted me. I stopped in my tracks.

Hampton was beside me. "Penelope, right?" It was moments like these that made me hate my parents for their name choices. Couldn't they have picked something—less of a mouthful? In this century? Boring?

"Penny," I corrected him.

"Sorry," he shifted. "I didn't get your number." I froze. Had I not just met this guy less than five minutes before? Introduced by a woman wearing clothing practically bursting from the seams? I'd been absent from the dating market for a few months, and it showed. My lack of a poker face made him laugh.

He shyly looked away and ran a hand through his hair. It was longish and looked soft. "Sorry. I know what that sounded like, and I really don't mean to be the wrong kind of guy."

"Then what guy are you exactly trying to be?"

He paused for a beat. "Mrs. Prickett assigned you to be my shadow buddy."

So, she made him run after me? *Creepy.* I eyed the door where students would soon begin to emerge. I was usually gone by this time, snuggled in my room, away from the world.

"Mrs. Prickett is a jokester. You'll see."

Good one, Penny. I looked over my shoulder, spotting my purple and white bike. *Good ole, Shirley.*

"It didn't seem like she was joking." Man, this guy was relentless. "I just don't know anyone. You're the first person I've met so far."

"Did she tell you to come and get my number?" I asked, trying to comprehend why the new star in school focused on me.

"Well, she said she had it," he said, "but I thought it might be better to introduce myself properly and to ask you."

"Aren't you from New York?"

He made a face, looking confused. "Yeah. Why?" I shrugged. Dad always said that we couldn't move to New York or the northern region because people weren't very nice.

"I just… didn't think New Yorkers were that considerate," I settled on.

"Isn't this the south?" he asked, a small smile tugging at his lips. "Aren't guys supposed to be, I don't know, all about chivalry?"

Touché. "Didn't you know that chivalry was dead?"

"Where I come from? Definitely," he said. Could he stop talking, like, now? Judging by the reactions that morning, I didn't think he'd have any trouble finding friends. And I wasn't an option. Even if I made myself one, Annie would make sure I wasn't.

I just nodded, not knowing how to respond. He also seemed unsure of what to do next. I could guess his thoughts: *Walk away slowly or pretend I'm getting a call from my mom, asking me where I went.* He chose neither.

"So, what do I tell Mrs. Prickett?"

Good point; what should he tell her? That I wouldn't cooperate in helping him jump to Annie's social status? Prickett would tell my parents. I could see her calling my mom's cell and telling her she was concerned about my wellbeing in school, sparking a whole lot of unnecessary parental conversations.

"You seriously don't want me as a tour guide," I said, readjusting the straps on my backpack. He raised an eyebrow, thrown off.

"And why's that?" The front doors swung open, and the bell rang. Students swarmed out, feeding my anxiety. I felt it ebb through my chest. Shit. This was exactly what I was trying to avoid. I tried to not glare at the pretty boy, who glanced at the students without a clue of how much it affected me.

A group of girls gathered nearby; they watched and whispered to each other. I'd bet money on what they were saying: *Why is he talking to her? He must not know what she did. Let's tell him.*

They were right about one thing: he would know sooner, not later. "Trust me on this one," I said, stepping back toward my bike. My bag felt heavier with each step. He was watching me. The gossip girls were watching me. The whole world was watching; my flight or fight instincts kicked in, and without a second thought, my legs moved faster. I reached for my bike. Shirley was ready to get going, too.

"What does that mean?" he asked, suddenly standing beside Shirley and I. This conversation had been going on for longer than I was used to. I didn't answer.

"Can you at least give me a reason?"

"Long story," I started to pedal.

"Wait, wait, wait," he said, putting up his hands. "I can't go back in there admitting that you didn't want to be my shadow buddy." Hampton paused, feigning seriousness.

"That would be embarrassing." People were officially watching us at that point, their phones locked and loaded as they took photos and texted. I'd been seen. No point in trying to dodge it.

He noticed, too. "Looks like you're a celebrity around here."

I met his eyes, careful not to fall into the greenish-hazel pools. "You have no idea."

"Seems like more of a reason to stick with you," he said. Actually, Hamp, the opposite.

But I thought of Mrs. Prickett and her imminent phone call to my parents: *"Yes, Mr. and Mrs. Brooks? Hi, Principal Prickett here. I'm calling with some concern regarding Penny. She seems to be having trouble—how do I say it?—re-emerging into her life after the accident. She refused to accompany a new student. Do you notice this type of behavior at home?"*

I bit my lip, knowing my cover would be blown if I turned down this kid's request. Mom would know that I wasn't actually going on a date with Dean (some kid I made up). I didn't even know a Dean. (In fact, I think it's on them for not catching that one). Dad would know that I wasn't actually going to parties on a Friday night but was retreating quietly to my dark room to watch Netflix in my closet. Call me a freak, but I called it innovative.

Basically, what I'm saying is, Hampton would ruin the facade I'd worked months to create.

"Fine," I said. "I'll do it."

"You sound like you're going to your execution."

"Please give me your phone before I change my mind." He handed it to me. I put my number in his contacts, contemplating for only a second the idea of putting in a fake number. That was one of Annie's favorite tricks.

"Thank you."

"I'd say anytime, but I think you know that I wouldn't mean it." My witty comeback surprised me; was I flirting?

"I figured that much, yeah," Hampton said through a grin. "Thank you for saving me from major humiliation."

I gripped my handlebars. "Do people ever tell you you're dramatic?"

"Maybe." He gave me this look, and I stared. He was good, I'll admit it. Other than with Jess, it was the longest conversation I'd had with someone my age in three months.

His name was suddenly called, and we both looked. It was his mom, waving to me with a smile and then gesturing for him to come. He turned to me, holding out his hand. "I'm looking forward to this friendship."

I stared, imagining what would soon be said about me:

"She's not good enough to even walk with him."

"Penny should be alone after what she did."

"The new guy is out of the question."

I held his hand for a moment, retreating. "We'll see about that." He crossed the front of the school and met up with his mom. I felt a flutter in my stomach, a foreign ounce of excitement. A conversation that may have lasted ten minutes made me feel things I hadn't felt since I made the mistake. Not even Jess could pull me out of my penalty box for longer than a few moments. I pedaled out of the school parking lot. The thing was, he *didn't* know, and just for a moment, I felt like my old self. But it didn't last long, and thoughts about what the following day would bring practically blinded my vision. There'd be stares, of course, and whispers of what *he* was doing with *me*.

Chapter 4

Shirley squeaked to a stop in my driveway, but I breathed in moments of delicious silence to myself. My house looked like it always did; the gray tiled roof paired oh-so-perfectly with the white exterior of the house, and the hanging Spanish moss from the huge tree hung over the majority of the property. I stared up at it, blinking at the cracks where sunlight managed to leak through. My dad hated the tree, always saying it was too messy. I even grew up listening to the complaints of the big, and ugly tree. I didn't understand why. I mean, look at it. The hanging moss provided the perfect shade for a sunny day, and plus, it was pretty. Anyone who said otherwise was just blind to beauty, I guess.

"Staring at that tree again?" I jumped, startled by Dad's voice. He wiped his hands on a dirty rag, dirt smudging his white T-shirt. He was smiling, shaking his head bitterly. I could practically see the twitch in his mouth, threatening to dive straight into why the tree caused more bad than good. The only reason why he didn't get his way and cut it down was because I loved it so much, but it didn't mean he was less bothered by it.

"Hi, Dad." I smiled and rolled Shirley into the garage, kicking out the kickstand and parking her in her usual spot. If you're wondering why I've assigned a name and pronoun to my bike, then blame my nine-year-old self. I named it when it was gifted to me, and I guess you could say that archaic names were a trend in the Brooks family.

Plus, Shirley has been a safe haven for me since the accident. Cars and I have a bit of a rocky relationship. I'll drive one, but I'd prefer not to. "How was school, honey?"

"It was great." I grinned, the muscles in my face stretching in a foreign fashion. You think I'm joking.

"Good!" He dropped the rag, seeming to be finished for his tasks of the day. Dad worked as a mechanic, so he was always messing around with his and Mom's car engines. Even when there was nothing wrong, I always joked with him about cars being his first love. "Anything interesting happen?" I took off my backpack, slowing and thinking of Hampton. Shadow buddy—Hampton. I wanted to roll my eyes, but the mystery boy was the perfect variable in keeping up the penny-show.

"I'm a tour guide for tomorrow," I started, trying to sound excited. But even to me, my excitement level was lame, and I worried he'd notice.

But he took a swig from his water bottle, nodding. "That's awesome, Pen."

I crossed the garage with an added bounce in my step and climbed the wooden stairs. "Oh, by the way." He stopped me, giving me a look. "Mom got a call from Mrs. Prickett." My stomach dipped. My bounce erased. Maybe it was good. Maybe she was telling her about my tour tomorrow and how things were really going great. I took another look at Dad's face, and it told me the opposite. Something was up. That bi—

He put his hands in the air in surrender. "Just wanted to warn you before entering the crossfires."

I gave a half-smile before walking, opening the door, and stepping into the house. Dad was always my buddy. Mom was at the kitchen counter, chopping something. The back of her head, blonde and streaked with light brown highlights, bounced slightly as she chopped. People said I was the spitting image of her, but I couldn't see it. She was Ms. Perfect. She always had her shit together. But at that moment, I felt scared for what was to come.

"Hi, Mom," I said, slinging my bag off my shoulder and letting it drop to the ground. She swung, the knife still in her hand, and I wasn't surprised to be met with The Face. It was a look I'd grown immune to seeing for a few months, just like she was immune to the disappointment called her daughter. But then her head would tilt to the side, just like it was doing then, and boom—it was the second part of The Face.

Sympathy.

"Mrs. Prickett called me," she started off, still giving me The Face. The corners of the lips turned slightly downward. Eyebrows drawn together.

I waited. My voice wasn't needed.

"And it turned into a pretty long talk." How long could the woman talk about Hampton? It was like Royal High acted as if he was the present-day Messiah.

"Sit down." She put down the knife, gesturing toward the table. Oh, no. Sitting was always a bad move. It meant something big was coming.

"Mom, whatever she said—"

"Sit." Her voice was firmer that time, so I sat. The wicker chair beneath me made the familiar cracking and stretching sound. I longingly eyed the hallway to the stairs, wishing I was in my bed with the curtains drawn.

Mom crossed the kitchen, stepping over the section of the floor that was broken.

They were planning on getting the kitchen redone soon; I just didn't know when. "How are you doing in school?" She gave me a hopeful look, almost like she was expecting me to say I was doing great and that I was actually planning on going to the first party of the school year that Friday.

"Fine," I said. "I told you I was doing great. School is great; my friends are better." I trailed off, hoping she'd get the picture and just lay off.

"Okay." She nodded, and I breathed a tiny sigh of relief until her lips parted and said, "That's interesting, considering Mrs. Prickett seems to think the opposite."

Was Mrs. Prickett out to ruin my life? God, she needed something else to bewitch. Like a dog. I should get her one. But an ugly one, because she didn't deserve a cute one. I stayed still, trying not to crack. "What?"

"She said that she's been watching you." She started slowly, and I knew it. She was obsessed with me. Stalker-level, grade: psychotic. I could file a restraining order. I wondered if that took long.

"That's so creepy."

"Penelope." When she used my full name, I knew it was time to pause. I watched her take a breath, almost like she was preparing herself for a battle. "She said she's been seeing you walking around alone in the hallways, looking pretty… removed."

"Removed?" I repeated.

"Removed." I didn't know what to say. "And she said you sit alone during lunch."

"That's not true; I sit with Jess every day."

"And that you made a special request to rearrange your schedule at the end of the day so you could leave a period earlier than everyone else." Okay, she got me on that one. If I wasn't so mad at Mrs. Prickett, I could've tossed her some points for her detective skills.

"I don't get it, sweetie." I looked up, noticing the small tremor in her voice. Was she... crying? Not crying, but definitely tearing up. She dabbed her eyes, confirming my suspicion. I hated making her cry. It was my third-highest guilt on the list.

"Your favorite time of the day was when you could leave with your friends. There were rarely days when you would be back right after school. Remember when you would all go and get ice cream?" Actually, Annie just loved leaving all together at the end of the day. She even had a meeting once with a teacher and made all five of us stay outside the room until it was done. And the ice cream was just an afternoon excuse to sit outside Creamy & Creamier Creamery and make fun of passersby. Again, another one of Annie's ideas. Wasn't she a gem?

"I really think we should talk about you going to live with Grammy." And there it was. The line I'd been waiting for—the threat I'd heard at least a dozen times.

"No." I shook my head, standing up. Her eyes followed me to the kitchen counter. "I told you that I was never going to live with her." Grammy was fine—great, even. She was the hippest grandma around. But it wasn't her that was the problem. It was the fact that I'd have to pack up my (read: more-than-slightly pathetic life) and move in with my grandmother, surrounded by her plethora of antique furniture and knick-knacks that covered nearly every surface imaginable. One time, she kept her outdoor Christmas decorations up until June. She explained she wanted to "continue spreading the cheer," but really, she just looked severely unhinged.

"The school year has barely started," she started, ignoring me and trying to reason. "You could transfer to a school in Arizona in no time."

"I'm not going!" I was at a near-yell, and it was then when the garage door swung open. What was it with parents practically ignoring your voice in arguments?

Dad stepped in. "What's all the yelling about?"

"Oh, nothing," I said, shrugging. "Mom just wants to ship me off to Arizona so she doesn't have to be the mother of the town's killer." The kitchen grew silent. A deadly silence that took more than usual to recover.

"Penny," Dad said, low.

"That's not true."

"But isn't it?" I rounded on them both.

"I'm the one that killed Jack Doe." Again, neither parent responded. They stared, and I think I unlocked a new level to my mother's face.

"*You* didn't kill him," she said.

"*I* was the one driving. *I* was the one drunk," I said in the same tone. "*I'm* the one that pressed the gas and hit him."

"That's enough," Dad said quietly. I knew I'd gone too far.

"I just want what's best for you," Mom said, a tear rolling down her cheek. She looked like she'd been slapped.

"Or what's best for you?" I mumbled, grabbing my bag and leaving for my room.

Chapter 5

Before ~ 11 July ~ A Time Between Drink 3 and 4

"He's over there," I grinned happily, my voice drowned by the music. Had it gotten louder? Definitely.

"Joy," Annie muttered next to me, taking a swig of her drink.

Heather approached us, growing equally as drunk as most of the junior class. "What took you guys so long? We missed you." Her high voice seemed to sound even more obnoxious, maybe having reached a new octave. Or tone. Or was it octave? Clearly, the vodka seemed to be intercepting the firing neurons in my brain. Annie gave me a look, stifling a laugh at my dumbfounded expression and our private, mean joke.

"What's so funny?" she asked, genuinely interested in what we were laughing at. "Is it Marcy Chapman's outfit? Did you see those shoes?"

No, we had not seen her outfit. But we nodded fervently, dropping some comments to sell our story. She seemed content, giving us both a quick squeeze before losing her concentration and following a boy who passed her view.

Annie and I giggled until arms suddenly wrapped around me. "Pretty girl," he murmured in my ear. He was tipsy at most, so definitely still in control. Justin was always in control; I'd only seen him once when he was super bad, but it was before we started dating.

I spun in his grasp, giving him my best smile. "J-man."

Justin laughed, throwing his head back. "I told you to never call me that."

"You said you liked it!" I laughed, too, giving him a pretend-pouty face.

He lowered his face, leaning down to my ear. "Just not in public." I rolled my eyes, pushing him a little.

"What are you drinking?" He peered into my cup.

I looked into the solo cup, giving it a swirl. "I'm not really sure. Annie made it. Want to try?"

Justin eyed it again, eyebrows drawn together for a moment. I touched his face.

"You okay?"

"Yeah." He smiled briefly, the dimples I loved about him popping out. I reached up on my tiptoes, giving him a quick kiss.

"Okay, love birds."

Annie came behind me. "Justin, it's girls time." I frowned; I was sure the girls wouldn't mind if I spent some time with him. His calm eyes lifted and met hers, holding for a moment before shifting to mine. I glanced between the two of them, still sober enough to understand tension.

His head dipped to mine, slowly and nonchalantly. "Be careful." Be careful. I made a face, almost wanting to laugh. Be careful with what, exactly? I was at a party with my junior class, stuck in the sleepiest town I knew. What did I have to be careful about? Drinking? But when his eyes flicked quickly to Annie, I wondered if it held a double meaning.

Or maybe it was entirely about one thing. One person.

Chapter 6

My room was dark and cozy, but the thought of leading Hampton around with surely four hundred and two pairs of eyes on me erased any ounce of drowsiness. I checked my phone, flinching once the artificial light hit my eyes. It was five thirty. I buried my face in my pillow. School wasn't for two and a half hours, but I figured I might as well get an early start to the day. Plus, I didn't want to run into my mom. Shirley was waiting. I rolled over, planting my feet on the shaggy carpet beside my bed. Today was the day I would get more glances than usual. I stood, heading to my bathroom. Another thought dawned on me: surely, Royal High students wouldn't allow my secret to be kept from Hampton. I closed my bathroom door, my hand lingering on the doorknob. Today was the day that another person would be told about Eric's party.

*

I was out the door without seeing either of my parents, so a relief for me. I pedaled out of the driveway and onto the street en route to Royal High. The sun was just starting to peak over the horizon, but it was still dark. If my parents saw me riding Shirley in the near dark, they would kill me. But I didn't mind. I liked any time of the day where the town wasn't alive yet, where the only creatures that stood in my presence were the early-rising seagulls.

I pedaled up a slight incline, turning down a road. I may have been an hour and a half earlier than the majority of the school, but who says I couldn't get some extra study time done? Time alone on my bike was soothing, especially in Port Royal. After getting through the October foliage of neighborhood trees and ordinary greenery, I reached the docks.

    The smell of salt and fish immediately set in the air around me; the fishermen were up and about, loading or unloading their boats. The docks were always one of my favorite places; people didn't come down there often because it wasn't the nicest attraction, but I liked it because of that. Sure, the biggest beauties were always important. But it was the small, even the least-important, things that ended up mattering the most. The wood of the dock sounded beneath Shirley's wheels, then stopped once I hit the smooth pavement and passed the fishermen docks. There was a shorter way to get to the school, but I liked the scenic route more. The sun was higher now, and my skin reflected a golden color. I sped up, not wanting to get stuck in the growing heat. Getting to school completely drenched was not part of my plan.

    I rode down a running and biking pathway, grains of sand having been blown onto the path. Shirley could take it, though, and we rode over it. I turned down a small, windy path, the familiarity of it aching in my belly. Since the accident, I discovered all kinds of hiding spots, but that one, down the windy path that people rarely visited, was one of my favorites. I reached a small clearing, the sound of water lapping calmly against the dark sand it touched, and dropped a leg to the ground. Shirley patiently obliged. I checked my phone time, knowing it'd be any minute until my distractions would visit. As if my little friends read my mind, a movie-worthy moment emerged: the five ducks turned a corner, making their way to the clearing. I'd like to think they knew I'd be here, considering I fed them around the same time every day. Weekdays, that was. I slept in on the weekends. But there they were, and I was already reaching for my bag. They quacked, not-so-quietly reminding me what was on the other end of our business deal.

"Okay, okay," I muttered, opening the zip-lock bag I prepared the night before. I pulled out pieces of stale white bread, ripping and tossing them. They grabbed the floating pieces quickly, chomping with sounds of satisfaction. Our business deal was simple: I fed them, and in return, they'd stick around and be my temporary distraction from the world. It was my sweet, little secret that I had myself a bargaining deal with small, aquatic birds. It beat getting wasted at some party. I tossed the remaining bread. They were peaceful, especially when they were babies a few months back. Oh, they were so cute.

I wasn't sure how much time I spent watching them bob in the water, the current rustling their paths. I sighed, crumbling the empty bag.

"Bye, guys," I reluctantly called over my shoulder, starting to pedal away. Trees rustled around me, and I spotted Royal High in the distance. I wanted to stop on the path and savor my alone time. But if I did, then it would take a lot for me to get back on track. I thought of my parents and the promise I made to myself the morning after Jack: use anything to continue forward because Jack didn't have that option. Keep going for Jack, and that included acting like I wasn't affected. A breeze blew a piece of hair into my face. It felt selfish, really. To have a breakdown over the suffering I'd caused Jack's family and possibly fall into a depressing hole that would take lots of work to emerge from. I straightened my shoulders, my spine cracking.

Hampton better be ready for his day of fun.

I parked my bike, not bothering to chain it up. Considering I lived in what I thought was the smallest town known to man—not New York City, no one would even bother to look at Shirley, let alone steal her. The school's doors were thankfully open, so I spent the next hour sitting in chairs outside of the office. It was where I'd be meeting Hampton anyway, so I could get ahead of work until then. Or at least pretend to.

"Penny?" a voice interrupted the silence of the hallways.

I jumped, startled. The snitch herself stood in front of me, a cup of coffee steaming in her hand.

"Hi, Mrs. Prickett."

She looked around the hallways as if expecting to see someone else. "What are you doing here?"

A big part of me wanted to be a smartass and say that I was a student, but thought it better not to. I smiled as sweetly as I could. "I just thought I'd get ready for my tour."

My principal didn't seem too convinced because, yeah, it was a pretty shitty excuse. But she nodded slowly anyway and said something even worse. "Well, why don't you come into my office? That way, you won't have to sit out here."

"That's okay," I started. "I'm fine here."

"I insist, Penny," she said, taking a sip of her coffee and gesturing toward the main office. "I should probably get you up to date on some new changes to being a shadow buddy. It's been a while for you, right?"

I gritted my teeth. *Only because your daughter was a raging bitch who ruined my social life and everything in between.*

"Okay. Thank you." *Not.* I stood with my bag, following her into the office. I tried to not stare at the snagged fabric on the back of her black and white striped business jacket, but it looked at me first, I swear. The school's receptionist smiled at both of us, wavering slightly once her gaze landed on me. Her red hair was tied tightly back into a bun, all uptight and strangled. It matched her personality.

"You can sit there." Mrs. Prickett pointed to one of the two chairs in front of her desk. I chose the other one just to annoy her. "So, are you excited for today? Hampton seemed rather content."

I nodded, trying to smile. My lips made a thin line instead, probably looking closer to a pained grimace than the bubbly smile she expected.

We sat in a few beats of awkward silence, her staring me down before I couldn't stand it any more. "You said there were changes?"

Mrs. Pricket nodded, blinking like she'd forgotten why I was actually there. "Right. He hasn't chosen a schedule yet, so you're not going to be showing him to his classes."

Oh, no. Please don't say it. "Instead, he's coming with you to your classes." *Was there even a God?* Now, I had to deal with even more eyes on me. Usually, a shadow buddy was responsible for showing the new student to each of their classes and then giving an excuse to be late to their own classes. So this was unusual.

"So how will he know to get to his classes once he gets them?"

She shooed it away like that meant nothing, turning to the window and pulling open the blinds. Beams of warm sunlight shone through, filling the room. "You know how that goes. He'll make some friends and then go from there." So, her philosophy was that he would make friends, and then they would show him around? Brilliant.

Maybe I should just hand him off to someone like Jess, or even better, Annie. That way, Mrs. Prickett would think I was with him all along. But she spoke up as if she'd heard my thoughts.

"I'll be checking in on you two today," she said, eyeing me. "Just to make sure everything is going well." I managed a nod.

"Penny, hon," Mrs. Prickett sat down, folding her hands across her desk and giving a tiny sigh. I stiffened, feeling like she was about to say something I wasn't going to like. "I know that things have been tough lately." Did she figure that out all on her own? Her tone changed from fake-cheery to real and deliberate. "But I want you to know that it *will* get better," she said, her tone trembling. Her eyes started to tear up, and I couldn't believe what I let myself get into. "Jack was a special boy, and people are hurting. And they'll hurt for a while." My chest burned. Just his name killed me a little more.

"But you need to come to the plate and own up to your mistakes instead of hiding away." I thought of the ducks this morning, wondering if she had any idea. Last time I checked, feeding ducks wasn't a crime. Her expression told me that I needed to get out of the room. "I believe that this life gives us lessons. That night was a lesson for you, and you have to deal with the consequences."

My eyes burned, but I refused to cry in front of her. What was this, some sort of intervention? Who gave her the right to lecture me on 'lessons' and 'consequences'? I tugged on a piece of my hair, tugging harder until my nerves protested in pain.

"This is a big year for colleges," her tone changed altogether, the sappiness gone and switching to something entirely different. "I won't let you take Annie down with you." What she meant was, "Stay at least fifty feet away from my daughter."

It felt like she'd punched me.

"Don't worry." I stood. The chair screeched against the floor. "I think she's already taken care of that for you." Without waiting for a response, I left the room and whisked past the mousy receptionist. I caught her eye, and I knew she'd been eavesdropping. I almost didn't care. I just wanted to be alone.

I passed Jack's memorial on my way, and I slowed. Just to dig the knife a little deeper, I punished myself and looked at it. Installed at the beginning of the school year, it was a glass case in the wall, brimming with academic and athletic awards, an honorary diploma that he would have been receiving this year, and a messy stack of written letters from students. A picture of him and Annie was pinned to the maroon velvet backdrop— Royal High's color. My throat burned in rage; all he was to her was a month-long hookup, and the fact she acted otherwise was a punch to his legacy. My glazed eyes flitted to the photo in the top corner, an older-looking picture that captured five grinning little kids. Maybe seven or eight years old. I'm in the picture, rosy cheeks and tanned skin indicating summer time. I didn't even remember that day. Some of the other kids were holding balloons in their hands, so it must've been some birthday party the class was invited to. I found Jack. His gleaming, goofy eyes inserted a choking sob in my throat.

I found the bathroom down the deserted hall, the lights finally on, and ready to welcome students. Pushing open the doors, I realized I was already crying. Hard sobs gripped my throat as I leaned into the sink. Hot tears streamed down my face, streaking the foundation I'd applied that morning. I flipped the faucet, water streaming and drowning out the sounds of my tears.

I was an ugly crier—Annie told me that. But how did anyone look good when they're crying? I wanted to tell her that. I didn't.

I put my hands under the water, a touch too hot. My brain screamed at me to pull them away, but all I could think of was the undeniable pain rushing to the surface. And the fact that, just for a moment, the hot water burned through the memories and feelings, and non-extinguishable repercussions. I jerked my hands away, my reddened skin seething. My tears still continued, though, and it took all of me to not crumble to the floor. Not only did she have to bring Jack up, but she also lectured me on my own healing process. Who was she to attack me?

I put my burning hands on either side of the sink, leaning and watching my tears fall into the rushing water. My wet hands gripped the counter hard. The burning pain somehow subsided. How could she throw him in my face like that? Assuming I hadn't taken responsibility for my mistakes, what did she know?

I took deep, even breaths, willing to slow my crying. I didn't need some kid walking in on Penny Brooks having a panic attack in the bathroom. In moments that may have taken a few minutes or longer, the tears stopped and left their mark. My eyes looked a shade of brown lighter, rimmed in remnants of angry black mascara and a red trail of aggravation. I swallowed, fishing in my bookbag for an extra makeup bag. I carried one at all times last year, so I hoped I hadn't taken it out. My hand grazed the familiar waxy bag. Bingo.

I went to work, spending the next ten minutes fixing what'd been ruined. Thank God my makeup skills hadn't gone rusty because, by the time I was finished, I looked good as new.

Well, almost.

There was nothing I could do about looking like a stoner except give it time. I checked my phone, knowing that the school was just about to be filled with kids. And Hampton.

I slipped my phone back into the side pocket of my bag, taking one last look at the mirror and deciding it was as good as it was going to get. Hampton was waiting.

Pulling open the bathroom door, I made my way back to the

office. Just as I thought, there were a good amount of early-comers milling around the hallways and lockers. Every step I took was like wading through water, but I'd made a promise.

And that promise was sitting beside the office, gazing at me curiously.

Hampton's eyebrows were drawn slightly together, feigning concern. By the time I reached him, he was already standing, his previous expression replaced with a smile.

"Good morning," he said, tipping his head to the side.

"Morning," I said, my tone scratchy. I swallowed, embarrassed. But he didn't even notice or pretended not to as he continued right on.

"You showed up."

I gave a half-smile. "You thought I wouldn't?"

Hampton gave a shrug, still smiling. "I had my doubts."

"I had pity for you. Thought I'd spare you the embarrassment." The banter was almost fun—*no*. I stopped myself. This was strictly a business arrangement. For my parents. For Mrs. Prickett. For college. A variable in moving forward.

He gave a laugh. "I'll forever be indebted to you, then."

I looked at him, unable to ignore what was so obvious. The cute smile. The cute face. The cute... okay, *everything*. His outfit even told me he was all ready for his first day of school, with khakis and a collarless polo shirt. I stopped my eyes from wandering. *Business arrangement, remember?* The warning bell rang, allotting the students five minutes. School was officially in full swing, but I already felt drained.

"Ready?"

Hampton nodded. "Lead the way."

Chapter 7

Spanish IV hadn't ever given me this amount of anxiety in my life, and I meant that wholeheartedly. I managed to ignore the looks on the walk to class, entertaining Hampton's easy chatter with a simple yes or no. After two flights of stairs and down the hall to the language classrooms, the amount of attention on me made me feel like a celebrity returning from rehab.

Hampton probably thought it was him, being the new student and all. I gave him a sideways glance, wondering what his reaction would be. His ever-present smile was still there, but a little smaller than it had been when he was alone with me. It hit me: Royal High's newest celebrity was shy. *Who would've known?*

I made my way to the corner seat. Jess didn't share my morning classes with me, unfortunately, so I wouldn't see her until lunchtime, which was going to be a whole other ball game.

Hampton followed, taking a free seat beside me.

I ignored the twenty sets of eyes trained on the both of us, spinning around and saying, "The teacher for this class is Señor Iban. He's cool; I like him." Señor was especially sensitive toward my situation, telling me on the first day that if I ever needed an extension, he would have no problem giving it to me. I didn't have the same treatment from other teachers.

He nodded. "Cool," and leaned forward in a whisper, "why?"

"Hey," the girl in front of me said, reaching an outstretched arm across my desk to reach Hampton. "I'm Hazel; it's nice to meet you."

I shrunk back, careful to not come in contact with her arm, which was protruding my personal space. *Seriously?*

Hampton eyed the close proximity, tentatively shaking her hand. The contact nearly brushed against my right boob. "Hampton. You too."

Hazel gave a warm smile, her eyes practically flashing with, *I'm-the-first-person-who-met-the-school-hottie-and we're-definitely-going-to-prom,* eyes.

Just then, the front door slammed shut, and Señor entered the room. The eyes of everyone receded, their new attention begrudgingly brought to our teacher. I couldn't help but see the whispering when he turned to write something on the board. It may have been the most brutal fifty minutes, so when the bell rang, I stood and hoped Hampton would follow without another glance back.

He seemed to get the message, though stopped to talk briefly with the teacher. I couldn't blame him, so while I held back and let everyone pass, the dirty looks were the cherry on top of a perfect class.

*

"Where are we going next?" he asked behind me. I slowed my pace, feeling bad. I was the worst shadow-buddy ever. We had already sat through Spanish and college writing, all complete with more distasteful looks. I wondered if Hampton noticed, but he didn't act like he did. Plus, guys never noticed anything.

"Sorry," I mumbled, deciding to glare back at a girl who was looking me up and down. "We're going to lunch. That's one of the best places." The window. That's all I loved about the stupid school.

"Awesome, I'm starving. Why is it one of the best places?"

I led him down two hallways and up a short flight of stairs. "You'll see." The day had been easier than I thought, actually. Apart from the lingering gazes, no one really tried to talk to me—just Hampton.

I pushed into the double doors. "Welcome to the coordinate plane." He gave me a confused look, fading quickly by the time he got a look at "Royal High's Biggest Attraction," a favorite line of Mrs. Prickett. What happened next could be described as a domino effect: every head, one by one, blurred into a pool of desperation as they turned their attention to Royal High's two most famous celebrities.

I swear, we could've been in a movie where a director said, "They're here! Everyone, look!"

"So it looks like there's," I paused, craning my neck to see the food that was being served, "spaghetti with meatballs." Pass. I didn't touch anything with meat. The room may have been my favorite, but the food wasn't.

Hampton nodded, grabbing a tray once we reached the stack. "Has this day been as bad as you thought it would be?"

I watched the kids in front of us move in slow motion, and all I wanted to do was get to the safety of our table and let Jess take over the conversations.

"Huh?"

He looked at me, blinking and turning his head back. "Everything okay?"

"Yeah," I said, looked at him. "Why?"

He watched me, looking like he wanted to say something but chose not to. "No reason. Just checking in." I felt myself squirm, weirded out.

We got our food, sidestepping some students who crossed our path, and he followed me toward the Eastside.

Just a few more steps, I told myself. *Almost in the clear*—someone I'd been waiting for stepped into our path, grinning at Hampton. We both stopped, and I had to give her credit—she held off for most of the day. He smiled a friendly smile, taking her in. I wasn't surprised he was subtly checking her out—find me a guy who wouldn't.

"Penny," the way she said my name seemed friendly to someone like Hampton, but to me, it was nothing of the sort. I knew her fake voice. I knew her bitchy voice. It was a combination of the two. "Why haven't you introduced me yet?"

I wanted to punch her. But instead, I gestured and said, "Hampton, this is Annie."

He shifted his tray to one arm so he could shake her hand. "Nice to meet you."

"Why don't you sit with my friends and I?" Hampton glanced at me, unsure. I smiled back, letting him know that I would have no problem with it. Letting him, I mean. Not I, no sir.

"Sure," he said. Annie said something chirpy back as we parted like the Red Sea.

I started toward my table.

"Penny," someone said my name. If my name was called one more time… I turned to Hampton, looking at me expectantly, a smile fading from something Annie said to him. "Where are you going?"

My mouth opened to respond, but nothing came out. It felt like the sound in the room dropped an octave, waiting for my next move. Annie's eyes narrowed behind Hampton, daring me to take a step and occupy a seat on the Westside. But Hampton was waiting, and what if Mrs. Prickett decided to drop by and see how things were going just to see that I'd abandoned him? I eyed the group of tiger sharks—*ahem*, girls—awaiting his arrival.

I took a tiny step in their direction, the room freezing. Or maybe it was just my internal organs. I avoided Annie's line of sight because all she could do now was just send aggressive cues with her eyes. Wouldn't want to be a bitch in front of the new hottie, would we? Still, I found a small amount of comfort in the fact that she was forced into silence by me.

I followed Hampton this time, led by Annie herself, to the Mets' table. My stomach churned. The last time I sat there was the final day of junior year, so it was weird, beyond weird.

We passed some tables on the Southside, their heads turning. I could guess what the collective thought bubbles would be: *Annie Prickett was allowing* her*?* I rolled my eyes. Call the newspapers; why don't you?

The girls I once called my friends were already looking up from their table, a territorial aroma radiating from their position. It was strange, having been so close with people and then... not. The switch-up was enough to give me whiplash.

"Annie," Claire, the suck-up, obnoxious brunet, commented. She said her name like it was an open-ended question, appointing herself as the official spokesperson for what the entire school wanted to ask: *what*, exactly, was going on?

Annie ignored Claire, though, something she did often, and patted the table instead. "Hampton, you can sit here." Hampton obeyed, sitting with his tray. I was still standing, staring down at the table. Hampton scooted over, patting it like Annie had done. A glint in his eye made me freeze; was he mocking her? Did he catch onto Annie's games? But whatever I saw was gone before

I noticed it, so I wasn't too sure.

The four girls, Claire, Jasmine (Jazz), Courtney, and Heather, all shared a look and leaned forward on their chins. Their brains probably screamed at them to be nonchalant, but I wanted to snort. They were anything but. If Annie and I were still friends, we'd trade glances and secretly laugh.

I swallowed, ignoring the gazes of the five girls that burned a hole in the side of my head. Clearly, Anna didn't make the cut. After a quick exchange of names, it was time for drilling.

"So, where are you from, Hampton?" It was Claire who asked, but I didn't dare look up. I stared at the brown spot on my apple, wishing I picked a different one.

"New York City," he said, swirling his fork in spaghetti and taking a bite.

Jazz heaved a dramatic sigh, "I would love to go there." Jazz was, without a doubt, the genuine definition of a PB&J. All Wonder bread, Jiffy peanut butter, and Smucker's grape jelly. Cut into diagonal slices. Wrapped in wax paper. You get the picture. She tried her hardest sophomore year to reinvent her literal PB&J status to a Met; the girl would've crawled the length of a marathon if it meant being a permanent member of the Westside. Annie didn't necessarily like her, but she appreciated her tenacity, at best.

"I've been there," Courtney said pointedly at Jazz, straightening her shoulders and looking right at Hampton. "Something we have in common."

"Court," Annie started with a tone that threatened to take her down. "Flying into JFK for a layover and then ordering a Shake Shack burger doesn't count." The other girls giggled, and Courtney shrunk. So it looked like Annie's personality hadn't changed. Or the table.

Hampton chuckled but added, "Shake Shack is great." Courtney perked up, but only a little, until she met eyes with Annie. She deflated like a balloon. I went back to staring at my apple, willing to disappear.

"New York was cool," he said. "But it was time for a change." His tone was strong. Impermeable. I looked at him, suddenly curious to know everything there was to know about him.

"Do you miss your friends?" It was Heather who asked this time, no doubt. No one could miss her high-pitched voice. Annie used to call her Squeaky behind her back. I wondered if she still did.

He nodded next to me, glancing at his plate and ripping the bread roll. We watched him pop a piece in his mouth. "Yeah, but we're keeping in touch."

"That's good," Annie said, sounding sympathetic but not fooling me. I knew her too well.

"Did you have a girlfriend?" And there it was. The question everyone was waiting to ask.

"Nope," he said, giving us all a shrug and looking at me last. We met eyes, and I went back to staring at the apple. Business arrangement.

I could definitely imagine the Queen Bee leaning a little closer and giving him a flirty look. It was her signature move, and now that she knew he was single and possibly ready to mingle, she silently called Dibs. "Why'd you move anyway?" What were these, twenty questions? Someone save me.

"Hey, girls!" Jess suddenly popped into the picture, interrupting the showdown.

She was then the center of everyone's attention. I could tell she felt just as uncomfortable with crossing to the dark side as I did, but she stood her ground better than I had. Even more, actually. I breathed a tiny sigh of relief; it felt good to have someone by my side.

"You have room, right?" she asked, and just when Annie said something like, "no," Jess didn't waste any time finding herself a spot. She shoved her way onto the bench that seated the four of them. Claire let out a sound of disgust, smushing the three girls next to her. When Jess was content, she folded her hands and grinned widely at the table.

It was way too weird. Annie, Jess, Claire, Heather, Jazz, Courtney, and me. All of us together again.

"So," Jess started, "what are we talking about?" I peeked at Hampton, who had this small smile, like he was clearly enjoying the show.

"Jess," Annie said with the same tone she'd said my name. "Aren't your friends on the Eastside missing you? Little rude to leave them alone."

"Aw, Annie," Jess said, her head tilting. She reached the short distance across the table, gripping Annie's resting forearm. Annie's face practically screamed at her to get off, but she remained still in the presence of Hampton. "That's so sweet of you to think of them. But no, they'll manage."

"Fantastic," she said back, pulling her arm back and dropping to her lap. I eyed her manicured nails, her pinky dangerously close to Hampton's thigh. The cutting conversation bordered full-on bitch mode, but they walked on eggshells because of the table's newest addition. I gulped down some air, feeling anxious from the table's nostalgia.

"Eastside?" Hampton questioned, crumbling his tissue and tossing it on his half-finished plate.

"The lunch room is divided into the four coordinates," Claire piped up, clearly motivated to get some talking time.

"Like math?" he asked, confused.

"No, like a compass," I said, soon snapping my mouth shut. Had I just talked?

Annie glared at me, tucking a piece of her bleached hair behind her ear. She started to point, swiveling on the bench. "The Northside is for teachers, usually. Students don't sit there." Her finger slid in the air, moving to the Eastside. "Eastside is for people without friends. The banished"—she glanced at me—"they usually stick to themselves."

I caught Jess's eye at the word 'banished' right before she said, "Right, Penny?" I inwardly rolled my eyes. I was wondering when she was going to start recognizing my presence in order to toss me some digs.

Hampton turned to me; his eyebrows pulled a bit together, but not saying anything. The table was quiet. It continued that way for only a few moments, but it felt like years.

Annie's finger then pointed to our table as well as all the tables along the huge window. I followed her finger, my eyes suddenly meeting Justin's. He blinked, probably confused as to why I was sitting with the Mets. I looked away, guilt swirling around. I was feeling way more that day than I was used to. I returned my attention back to my spotty apple.

"We're on the Westside right now," she raised an eyebrow, giving a small smile. "You'll catch on to the type of people who sit here." I snorted in reflex.

Annie glared at me. "Something to add, Penny?"

Jess plucked a piece of Annie's hair, completely derailing the conversation away from me. "I love this color, Annie. Remember that time in freshman year when the hairstylist accidentally dyed your hair *orange*? And you had to wear that

hat to school, like, every day for a month until—"

"No," Annie said, her jaw clenching. "I don't."

Hampton cleared his throat. "And the Southside?"

"PB and—" she started, stopping herself and looking at me for a split second. I had come up with the name a few years ago, and it stuck. "Basically, the kids who will never leave Port Royal. Born and raised. They have their own group."

"Gotcha," he said, looking at me. "Where do you usually sit?" The question may have derived from genuine curiosity but also a hint of something else. Almost like he was directing his attention to me because he knew it would bother her... no. That was crazy.

Jess saved me before I had to figure out an answer, changing the subject. "We haven't gotten a chance to meet yet. I'm Jess."

"Hampton," he shook her hand.

"Penny's my best friend," she explained her sudden appearance, winking at me. "She was really excited to be your friend for the day."

I half-choked on my sip of water, coughing.

"Yeah?" Hampton questioned, turning to me. The corners of his lips tugged upward. "I never would've guessed."

Annie cleared her throat. "That's also something I was wondering about. Who, in their right mind, let *you* be the person to show him around?" **The golden question I was waiting for.**

My face burned, and I stared straight at her, trying to find an excuse.

"We ran into each other," Hampton filled in like it was no big deal. "And Principle Prickett suggested it."

Annie's face dropped, her eyes practically darkening. "Principle Prickett... *suggested* it?"

He nodded. She mashed her lips together, looking down at

her plate and probably wondering why her own mother didn't think of her daughter to show him around.

The table was quiet until familiar-sounding heels clicked over toward our table, revealing the woman of the hour. Please join the party. "Ladies! I'm glad you could all meet our newest student." She did say she'd be checking in, but could she have chosen a worse time to visit?

"He's great, Mom," Annie said, and Hampton looked at me, catching on to the mother-daughter scenario. "I think he'll make a great addition to Royal High."

She asked me a few questions about which classes we'd been to already, then switched to Hampton to ask him a few more. I gave bland answers without much detail, still not over our conversation from the morning. Jess and I swapped a few looks, communicating telepathically. We had so much to discuss: Hampton, Mrs. Prickett, Annie, and even Justin.

The bell sounded overhead, interrupting his conversation.

"It looks like it's time for Lit," I pushed myself up from the table, waiting for Hampton to gather his stuff and follow. I didn't bother saying anything else to my principal, considering we had had enough to talk about for the day. She got the message, waving goodbye to the group of girls and retreating.

"It was nice to meet you all," Hampton said, eyes flicking quickly over each of them. They returned the gesture, turning to whisper to each other once he turned away.

Annie's manicured hand grasped his wrist. "There's a party this Friday. Back-to-school celebration, or whatever," she rolled her mascara-coated eyes, feigning disinterest. "You should come." I could practically see her hazel eyes flashing with her plans to rip his clothes off.

Hampton nodded, genuinely looking interested. "Cool. That

sounds fun."

"Be my partner in pong?" she asked, giving her best version of a sweet smile.

The other girls traded some glum glances behind her back; at the slightest, they wanted to get a taste and steal some minutes of his time. But Annie was quick, and no one would *ever* defy her. Unless they wanted to be me. He nodded, saying something I didn't quite catch. I knew that Jess was planning on going, but could you take a guess at what my plans were? Netflix and popcorn. Maybe some late-night visits to the ducks. They traded one last smile, and then he followed Jess and I to the huge trash can.

"That was... fun," he said, tossing his trash and stacking the trays with the others. I hid my small smile, not sure if he was being serious or entirely sarcastic.

Jess was watching me, giving me a look. I mouthed, "What?"

She just shrugged, stacking her tray. "Nothing. English Lit, anyone?" Thank God Jess shared the next class with me.

Chapter 8

It was late one night, just after I finished dinner with my parents, and retreating to my room when he called.

I stared at the caller ID for so long that I was surprised it didn't go to voicemail. What could he possibly want? "Hello?"

"Hi," his familiar voice, once comforting, reminded me of everything that had happened with us. His tone was soft.

"Justin," I swallowed, shifting in my bed and sitting up. My loose hair fell over my shoulders, hanging limp. "What's going on?"

"Nothing. Nothing, I just…" he trailed off, and I heard him move. "I saw you sitting with Annie the other day. And I know you showed Hampton around."

What was this, some sort of confrontation? I pressed the phone harder to my ear. "So?"

"I'm just trying to see if you're okay."

"Why wouldn't I be okay?"

"C'mon, Pen." He sighed. "We're not playing this game."

I pulled the blanket up over my lap. "I don't know what you're trying to do right now. You're first worried about me being an introvert, and now you're concerned that I was sitting with my old friends and helping a new student out?" He was quiet, and I was on a roll.

"What are you trying to get out of this, Justin?" I asked. "I mean, you call at least once a week and ask the same question."

"I just care about you," Justin said, his voice soft. "And I still... love you." I shut my eyes, welcoming the darkness behind my eyelids. I knew he did. A warm feeling climbed into my chest, pushing me to say it back. But then I thought of Jack. And the disappointment on Justin's face. And I wished that I could say the same back because I did love him, but it felt different. Tainted. Damaged by me. I didn't deserve to be loved by Justin or carry on like someone didn't die and wouldn't ever feel again. Every time I looked at Justin, I found myself being reminded of every bad decision I'd made that night leading up to the climactic event.

"Penny?" He searched for a response. For anything, really. But I couldn't. Not then, not ever again. I'd already broken enough people's hearts. I wasn't about to add Justin to the list. "Do you remember what I said to you that night?" *Did I remember?* I remembered more than I wanted to. I rarely blacked out from alcohol, something that obviously proved to be a curse. I would do anything to forget the majority of that night. I shut my eyes, the sound of his steady breathing forcing me into a drowning memory.

"Shots!" My slurred voice contradicted my request as I raised the plastic bottle of vodka above my head. Music thumped rhythmically through speakers in the ceiling, bouncing off walls and coaxing our junior class to ignore the dread of an upcoming school year and just dance. And flirt, drink, and ignore the fact that it was nearing two a.m. on a Saturday night.

Justin placed a hand on my lower back just as laughter erupted along with applause from my friends. "I think you've had enough."

I stuck out my tongue, rolling my eyes. "Party pooper."

His calm brown eyes blinked before turning to our friends. "How much has she had?" I wanted him to have fun too.

Regardless, my selfishness proved to become the first mistake of the night.

"Shots or drinks?" Annie asked, grinning and leaning into her newest conquest. Despite her remarkable ability to shut feelings on and off and her complete lack of regard for treating boys as human beings, we loved Annie. Besides, Jack didn't object. He placed an arm around her shoulder and took a swig of his drink.

Justin stared at her, not appreciating her attempt at being funny. She rolled her eyes. "I lost count. Who cares?" She gave a smirk like a period to the end of a sentence. I locked eyes with my best friend. Through our shared drunkenness, we burst into laughter. Maybe it was the look on Justin's face. Or the way Jack was staring at her, practically daring her to undress.

I shrugged, turning and putting a hand on Justin's face to keep him steady. Or keep myself steady. "If I'm being honest, I lost count of how many drinks I've had tonight." The rest of us laughed, except for Justin, who glanced at me worriedly. I couldn't count the number of times he'd given me that look.

"You're cut off," he mumbled in my ear.

I pulled back, challenging him by raising the bottle high. "Who's gonna stop me?" Annie, Jess, Jack, and the rest of our friends cheered. I was Party Penny; I had to keep up with the set standards.

Unscrewing the cap, I tossed it to the floor and lowered the bottle to my lips.

"Penny," the tone of Justin's warning resonated.

Annie gave me a low thumbs up and tipped her head as if to say, "What are you waiting for?" I joined a chug countdown in the room, with the chorus beginning at ten. The crowd reached 'five'—so close—when the bottle was ripped from my hand by someone resembling my boyfriend. Vodka spilled. Someone would have to clean that up in the morning. Not me. It was never me.

Justin shook his head angrily, leaning close to me. "What are you doing?"

I swayed harshly and put a finger to his lips. He was so cute, but he'd ruined my shotgun. "What is your deal?"

"What's my deal?" he asked as he jabbed a finger to his chest, then shook his head again. I frowned. I'd upset him.

Annie stepped between us. "Time out, lovebirds." She looked at Justin. "Justin, chill. She's just having fun," she said, adding, "It's summer," like her case was sealed. I could tell he wanted to say something back, something snarky to put her in her place, but that wasn't Justin. He wasn't confrontational in the slightest. And Annie knew it. She smiled at him, daring him to speak, but he just stared at her with an angry glint in his eyes.

"Penny," his voice brought me back into the present, to where my life was not at all like it was before. I sat frozen in my bed. I was startled; the memories were strictly and usually sanctioned to my dreams, appearing with scary and perfect vividness. Not sparked by something.

"I have to go," I said. "My mom is calling me."

Justin didn't say anything. "Okay. I'll see you at school." I hung up, tossing my phone to the foot of my bed like it was on fire. My heart hammered against my chest, fear trickling over my skin. Was this a new thing now? To be thrown into memories not projected through dreams?

I swiped my water bottle from my nightstand, taking a sip. I thought of the way I'd hung up on Justin, attempting to distract myself from one awful subject to a depressing one. Sure, you could call me a bitch for treating him the way I did. I'd been called one when I was a Met—I *was* one when I was a Met. But I was doing Justin a favor, so why couldn't he get that through his head? Couldn't he see that I wanted nothing to do with him? With anyone?

*

I spotted Jess the next day at her locker, walking to where she stood and heaved a sigh. She eyed me, putting in a book and exchanging it for another. Her hair was down, spread over her shoulders like a shiny fan. She always looked good for school, ready to walk down any runway. Since I was practically invisible, I didn't see a point in putting in as much effort as I used to. I mean, would you put on your best jeans and concealer for a solitary walk in the woods? My point is exactly.

"You look like shit," she commented, handing me her iced coffee. "I think you need this more than me right now."

I grumbled, taking it despite my ill-feelings toward coffee. "Thanks. I barely got any sleep last night."

She shut the locker door, and we walked in the direction of class. "Why?"

I glanced at her. "Justin called."

"Again?"

I nodded. We pushed into the double doors at the end of the hallway, turning a corner. "I just don't know what he wants from me. I've made everything pretty clear."

"Yeah…" she trailed off, staring straight ahead.

"Jess," I said. "What?"

Her shoulders rose and fell, looking like she was deciding something. "I was going to tell you, anyway."

I was no longer part of the steady stream of students. "Tell me what?"

"He told me he wants you back." I looked at her, my expression neutral. "Why are you looking at me like you already knew that?"

"Because I do," I said, my tone insinuating that she knew already. "Didn't I tell you?"

"No, you didn't." I felt guilty almost instantly; had I really made up this whole scenario in my mind when I told her? Before, I was telling everyone and dissecting every annoying detail. But then, standing in front of Jess with people rushing past us, I answered my own question: no, I didn't tell her. In fact, I don't remember the last time I told her something substantial.

"We're gonna be late for class," she murmured, ducking her head. I followed, unsure of what to say. No, that's not right. I knew what I needed to do—apologize. Apologize for everything.

Later that week, Hampton earned his seat on the Westside. For the first few days, it was with Annie and the girls, but by the end of the week, he migrated to the guys' table, parked right next to Justin. I'd peek over from my Eastside table and catch them talking, sometimes laughing.

Needless to say, Hampton Prescott was thriving. Like I cared. "You're staring," Jess whispered in my ear.

I jumped, her laughter following. "Shut up." She grinned, shaking her head, and starting back on her sketchbook. Jess's artistry was so insane that she deserved to skip art school and dive straight into the business.

"What under-appreciated animal is it today?" I peered over her shoulder, trying to sneak a peek. Jess had a passion, I'd say, for random animals no one—literally no one—had ever heard of. Sure, she had always been a fan of animals to begin with. But something about her intensity with sketching forgotten animals, bringing them to the light in a fantastic array of lines and shading, was sort of beautiful.

Jess grinned proudly, tilting the sketch toward me. "Fennec fox." When I didn't respond immediately, or at least make an attempt in faking my knowledge for fennec foxes, she heaved a sigh and pulled the sketch back to her. "Classic."

"How am I supposed to know what that is?" I popped a chip into my mouth, chewing and trying to contain a small smile. "It looks like"—I eyed the tiny face and the one huge ear she finished shading—"like that elephant." I snapped my fingers, "like Dumbo."

She puckered her lips, giving the same face you'd give a wiggly puppy. "It's so cute."

I watched her shade the fox's almond-shaped eyes, and I realized that Jess was someone who always stood up for the ones who didn't get enough attention. I stopped mid-chew, my gaze dropping to the potato chips held in my hand. Was I like the fennec fox? Someone she believed she had to stick up for? Save? Sketch and shade and perfect, until I was ready to be seen alone—without an artist to stand in as support? I swallowed the chip, leaving a bad taste in my mouth.

"I submitted my application yesterday."

"For Parsons?" I smiled for real. "Did you submit the art portfolio too?"

"Not yet."

She seemed further hunched over her piece, sketching thoughtfully and lighter.

I flicked her, "Are you crazy? Why!" Jess rubbed her shoulder. "Ow."

"That did not hurt." I laughed.

"You know I have sensitive skin."

"Jess," I started, completely abandoning my chips. "Design is all you've ever wanted to do. Just take a look at your room." One weekend, when her parents were away on some anniversary vacation, we—the Mets, crashed in her room and stayed up too late every night, eating bad cupcakes and drinking even worse cocktails. Jess decided her room was too boring, pulling out all the paint she had. Her once-white walls became tattooed in whatever drawing came to her mind. We all wrote our names, and since we weren't artists ourselves and got bored, Jess still continued the job after we left. Her parents weren't exactly thrilled that their daughter's pristine room had been covered by our disorderly contributions. Jess ended up continuing our artwork, but definitely in a more refined manner.

"Oh, come on. Anyone can do that," she said, her tone a little smaller than I was used to. I knew she wasn't exactly overconfident with her work, but it was always strange for me to see Jess's loud personality dimmed so harshly. "You guys helped too, remember?"

I snorted, packing up the chips and taking a sip of my water. "We wrote our names. And then got pulled into stories of some stupid guy that Annie was obsessed with at the time."

Jess rolled her eyes. "Right, right. Rob-something?" She finished the last of her ham-on-wheat sandwich, brushing off any crumbs that may have landed on the fox. I nodded. The cafeteria was louder than usual today, with the Westside contributing to most of it.

"You have to submit it. What are you so afraid of?"

She responded with a pointed look, tipping her head toward the Westside. "I can ask you the same thing."

I shifted in the wooden chair. "What are you talking about?" I knew exactly what she was talking about.

"Hampton. I see you look over there all the time," she raised her recently waxed eyebrow. "If you want to talk to him, then go over there and talk to him."

"Oh, yeah. That sounds like a swell idea. Nice thinking." I could see it now: Annie staring me down, whispering to Hampton, the Mets, and everyone. Plus, why on earth would I want to talk to him?

Jess just gave me one of her knowing smiles, shrugging and starting to pack up her work. I watched her carefully slip the fox into a leather folder.

"I'll make a deal," Jess said, holding out her pinky. "I'll submit my portfolio to Parsons…" She paused for a dramatic effect. "If you talk to Hampton." I scoffed.

"Something tells me that your future is a bit more important than some kid that everyone will forget in a few months."

"Wow, harsh," she said, putting a hand to her heart to feign pain. "How do you think Hampton would feel if he knew you talked about him like that?"

"Why do you think I'd even want to talk to him?" I ignored her, glancing over to the Westside. Hampton threw back his head in a laugh. He returned, saying something, until his eyes fell on mine. It was one, delicious moment, but that was all it took for me to turn away.

"Maybe because you two just undressed each other with your eyes."

My mouth fell open. Undress? That was a bit far. Way far. I was curious, I'll admit. I'd had a taste of the school's celebrity, but we hadn't spoken since the tour. The more I watched him, though, in the span of a week since I'd met him, it was beginning to become clear that he was just like every other high school kid who faked it till they made it. Wasn't that all that high school was? Just a temporary stomping ground to get through, complete the credits, and get on your way to the rest of your life?

Jess whistled, waving a hand in front of my eyes. "Pen-pen, you in there?" I grabbed her hand, pushing it away.

"Yes, I'm here."

"Did I interrupt your wet dream?"

My mouth fell open again. I fake-glared. "I'm leaving."

"No, I get it."

I packed up my things, swinging my bag on my back. I spun back to her, only to have found her wiggling her eyebrows.

"You want to be alone with those thoughts."

I hit her, shaking my head and starting to backtrack. "Submit the portfolio."

"You know my deal," Jess sang, resting her chin in her hands. There was no way she was going to bet her future on a conversation with Hampton and I. Right?

Chapter 9

It was that Friday morning when another part of my life decided to implode.

I bounded down the steps, my white sneakers slapping against the wood. I made my way through the dimly lit hallway and into the kitchen. It was growing bright, the sun rising and peaking through the white flowy curtains above the sink. I grabbed a cup from the cupboard, filling it with water from the fridge. The window was open ajar, a breeze drifting through and ruffling the stillness. Some of the bills slid across the granite-topped island, and my mom rushed to collect them.

"Penny," she started, stacking them. "Your dad and I wanted to talk to you before you went to school." I shut my eyes for a moment, just wanting to have gotten through the morning peacefully and without a formal hearing. If only Mom had adopted this method as much as Dad had; he knew when and when not to bother me. We were close like that. Mom, on the other hand, clearly did not get the memo.

The water overflowed the glass cup, spilling onto my hand. I sighed dramatically, moving to dry it up.

"Penelope? Did you hear me?"

"Yes, Mom," I said, wiping my hands off and turning to her. "Where's Dad?"

"In the—"

"Right here." The man himself stepped through the garage door, smiling at the both of us. "How are my girls this morning?"

"Good." I gave him a smile, hoping he'd buy it. He usually did. I watched him kiss Mom on the cheek.

"John, remember how we wanted to talk to Penny?" This was usually how her questions went, starting with, "John, remember this?" or a "John, remember what you thought of?" All in all, maybe he could look like the bad guy for once.

Dad pulled the orange juice from the fridge. Nodding to me, he said, "Sit down for a sec."

"I have to go to school," I said. Please, let me just go to school, where I can disappear in a whole other way. But he only let out a short whistle, pointing to the high chair sitting on the island. I sat, knowing there was no way out of this. I held back an eye roll at the familiar setup: Mom and Dad sitting in front of me, preparing to have a conversation regarding my wellbeing. Mom's hands were usually folded in her lap, a rigid posture adorned with The Face. Dad at least tried to appear more casual, with his head tilted and one leg bent over his knee.

"How did that tour go? With the boy?"

Tour? Hampton? What does he have to do with this? And that was more than a week ago.

I made a face, shrugging. "Fine. It went fine."

"Was he nice?" she was prying, her eyes trained on mine.

I looked back and forth between the both of them. "Just tell me what you really want to talk about." It was quiet for a little bit until Mom's hard gaze flicked at Dad. He took a breath.

"We've been talking," he started, scratching his head. Uh oh. Did Mom finally convince Dad to ship me away? Or maybe they finally decided to let me homeschool. I smiled a tiny smile to myself, knowing it was that. Perfect, "And we think you should start seeing Dr. Yao again."

My face fell. "What?"

"We never should have stopped in the first place, and we think you were making progress when you were with her." Dr. Yao. The therapist. I got her almost immediately after the incident, and yeah, she may have lightened the load a bit, but she could never erase that night. No one could.

"What is going to make you guys understand that I am *fine*?" My voice was rising, anger boiling.

"Lower your voice, young lady," Mom said, her tone borderlining an octave where she'd lose it. She glanced at the open window. Oh, but of course. So the neighbors didn't hear the crazy girl yelling. I struggled to contain a mocking laugh. Mom's top priority was maintaining the perfection of a household that only contained 2/3rds of it. Oh, the tragedy.

"And you may be fine," Dad said, his tone reasonable and calming. "But it's just some support."

"I don't need support. I just want to be left alone!" I stood, the chair scraping against the floor. I was losing it; I knew I was. But I took a steady breath, knowing I had to keep it together so they wouldn't crack what I had worked so tirelessly to keep complacent.

"And that's the problem, now, isn't it?" Mom said, her hands then raised from her lap, laying flat on the table. I could tell she wanted to stand and reach my level, but I could practically see her inner voice screaming at her to stand her ground. "You will go to Dr. Yao whether you like it or not, Penelope. It's either this or Grandma's."

My mind raced; how could I get out of both? I did everything I thought possible to stay under the radar: stay out of trouble, maintain a steady-grade point average, and okay, lie about my popular social life. "None of this was your fault," Dad said, his eyes soft.

"How can you say that?" I stared, my hands beginning to shake.

Dad stood, trying to reach out to me, but I dodged him.

"Someone is *dead*. Because of me." Mom tried to not flinch.

"Sweetie, we just think Dr. Yao is the best option right now to help you move past all this."

"What makes you think I'm not moving past it?" I asked, feeling impulsive. "Besides, I'm going to a party tonight. A back-to-school party."

"You go to parties all the time…" Dad trailed off. He was right; I forgot I lied to him about all the parties I'd been 'regularly' attending.

"This is different," I said. "It's at Eric's house." They stopped, looking at each other. I almost wanted to say, "Hah!" but I couldn't because I just screwed myself over. "I'm going to school," I ducked my head, pulling open the door to the garage. I found Shirley, grabbed her, and rode out in the direction of school. I operated Shirley in an autopilot manner; the change in elevation from driveway to ground startled me. What had I just done?

"Fuck," I said under my breath, pulling onto a sidewalk. That was the only thing worth saying.

Chapter 10

I found myself pacing my bedroom, the sun on its downward trend in the sky. I knew I solved the issue with my parents, at least temporarily, so that was squared away. I nibbled at my nails, the newly painted polish surely coming off. Ask me if I cared, because the only thing I could think of was the impending doom I was sure to be facing in a few hours.

Crowded hallways filled with my classmates.

Blaring music so loudly, it seemed to shake the bones of the house. Drunk guys, getting too close for comfort.

Drunk girls staring me down, wondering why the public shunning wasn't enough.

The smell of cheap beer and vodka oozing from the pores of girls who sprayed too much perfume over themselves and guys who attempted to use cologne for the first time.

Walking into the same house where I'd let everything get too out of hand.

A knock interrupted my pacing, followed by Jess stepping tentatively into the room. "What did I just walk in on?" She raised an apprehensive eyebrow, dropping her bag to the ground. It was ready to burst, filled with essentials for the night.

I walked to the opened door behind her, shutting it softly. "I'm having a major setback."

"What?"

I dropped my voice to a whisper, "I really don't know if I can do this. I mean, Eric's house?"

She looked like she was debating her answer, biting her lip. "You won't know if you can do it unless you try, right?"

"Everyone will be there." Annie. Her minions.

"Yeah, but," she stepped around me to my makeup desk, "you know who'll be there too?" I stared, waiting.

"Hampton Prescott."

I rolled my eyes, crossing the room to my bed and sinking into it. "So?"

"Well, if I remember our deal correctly..." she trailed off, unzipping the makeup bag and pulling out concealer and lotion. She uncapped the lotion, beginning to apply it to her cheeks.

"I don't know why talking to him is so important to you." I mean, the possibility of us was impossible. Annie would never allow it. The student body would never allow it. I wouldn't allow it.

I watched her shoulders rise and drop quickly. "You have submitted, though, right?"

"You have talked to him, right?"

I sighed. She had to have submitted it; there was no way.

"Assuming you haven't picked out an outfit yet, I'll do it for you." She stood, still rubbing in the primer, and reaching my closet. It took me an hour, maybe even more, to choose the perfect clothes. Eventually, I settled on a pair of black skinny jeans, sneakers, and a gray halter top. I said no to all the flashy and bright-colored articles of clothing; I wanted to blend in, not stand out. It was funny—my flashy clothes assisted what I was driven by most: to be seen. Now, I couldn't think of anything worse.

"Okay," she said, pulling back the mascara wand to survey her work. "You're ready." My stomach dipped, mimicking the feeling of being on a rollercoaster. Trust me, my life lately could have fooled me, too.

After gathering what we needed, we both made our way downstairs. The kitchen lights were dimmed, and the smell of Mom's baked chicken hung in the air. Mom and Dad sat in the living room across from the kitchen, the TV playing lightly in the background. Mom watched the TV, some cooking show playing, while Dad read. I asked them once why they didn't just choose something they could watch together, but their answer was simple—to them, at least.

"We like to be together, even when we're doing different things," Dad said with one of his goofy smiles, winking at me.

Jess and my entrance stirred the semi-silence in the living room, and they both looked up. Dad snapped his book shut, seeming to be happy about the distraction.

"Off to the party?"

We both nodded, Jess adding, "Yep!"

Mom uncurled her legs, "Do you need anything before you go? Cash? Food?" Wow, I could practically see the excitement in her eyes.

It took everything in me to not say, "Sure! Want to take my place?" But I shook my head instead.

"When will you be home?"

"Make sure it's way past a reasonable hour," Dad interjected, shooting me a look and waving his book in the air. "And I want you to join a biker gang, too. The both of you. Should build character."

Jess laughed, and okay, I gave in and smiled.

Mom shot him a look, so small that only I noticed, but it made me feel more inclined to like his joke. By the time we left, it took Jess all of three seconds to crank the music and roll down the windows.

Jess chirped away, probably her attempt at distracting me from the fact that, yes, I was actually sitting in a vehicle. It helped a little. I'd only been in a car a handful of times since the accident, but it wasn't an elective decision. Doctor's appointments. Grocery-shopping. Places too far to ride Shirley to.

I clicked my seatbelt in, sitting back into Jess's tan leather seats. "Remember Annie would never let us roll down the windows or play the music too high?" I nodded, silent among the music that seemed to be getting higher. Her philosophy was that the wind would ruin her hair, and the music would make us look like we were trying too hard. I never really understood where she was coming from, considering it was clear as day that everyone looked up to her. *Was Annie... less put together than she made it seem?* I shook my head to myself, feeling stupid for thinking such a thing. Annie was the queen of confidence.

Jess clicked on her blinker, turning onto Cove Street. The car sped up a little, the outside flashing by faster than Jess's normal driving speed. I eyed the sickening, all-too-familiar street; the two traffic lights loomed in the distance, with the same line of perfectly trimmed trees alongside the road. Each was luscious and green, always being fed by landscape workers, except one that stood out to me like a sore thumb. Tucked away and seeming smaller than the others, it was browning. Dying.

I swallowed, feeling like the browning tree. Knowing what it felt like to be dying on the inside, but expected to be in pristine condition because the people around me were. I gripped my seatbelt, pulling it tighter over my chest as the events of Cove Street started to peak in. *Had I gotten so pathetic that I started to sympathize with a tree?*

By the time we flew through the green light, I let go of a

breath I hadn't realized I was holding. Jess pretended she didn't notice, but she had to know that I hadn't been on Cove Street since Eric's last party.

She turned down the music a notch, saying in a sing-song voice, "We're almost there!" It was light, though—not so much so that it would freak me out. But even so, I knew we were almost there.

"I'll be with you the whole time," she promised, slowing behind a line of cars parked on the street. Even from our spot, I could already hear the thumping music. I looked at her, managing a nod and a smile. God, I deserved an Oscar for my acting. We got out of the car, Jess leading the way with her long legs and easy stride. I followed behind, trying to ignore the tightening in my chest. I reached behind my back, pinching some of my hair between my fingers and pulling.

"Hey," Jess called out, waving a hand to some people who milled around Eric's driveway. I expected them to look, stare even, and wonder what the hell I was doing there, but they didn't.

Maybe they just didn't recognize me.

We walked up the steps, and soon I found myself on the same platform that sparked the disaster of events. It took the wind out of me (while I never really knew what the saying meant, I knew then).

I tugged my hair harder, a memory washing over me. My vision blurred.

"I'm not really hungry," I said again, my voice feeling far away. I was too fixated on Justin being pissed at Annie and barely looking at me. He retreated into the crowd of my classmates, and I followed Annie and Jack outside to the front steps.

"I'm always hungry," Jack said, slinging an arm around Annie's small waist and pulling her to his side. Annie rolled her

eyes, looking to the side and looking pissed at me. Her angry hazel eyes looked glazed, and I wondered if she'd done anything additional to drinking. Nevertheless, she looked at me expectantly. They'd been wanting to go to McDonald's, but I was too preoccupied with the fact that I'd upset Justin. And Annie was mad at me for being too wrapped up in Justin's feelings.

"Just come, anyway." She gave me a look that I read as Don't-Leave-Me-Alone-With-Him-I'm-Not-In-The-Mood.

I sighed. It was coming close to the four-week mark with her and Jack, meaning she was almost done with him. "Why don't we just find something inside? Eric must have food in the fridge somewhere."

Annie whined like a nine-year-old, taking a step toward me. Despite her completely trashed balance and physical state, she was still as perfect as ever. Her carefully applied mascara was still intact, outlining her hazel eyes, which rolled again in annoyance.

"You just want to be with Justin, don't you?" She said it like she was accusing me of something.

"No," I said quickly. "I just think we're too drunk to drive and get chicken nuggets right now, that's all."

"It's Port Royal. You know this place dies at eight." I didn't respond, still not sold.

She was right, but it still didn't feel good to get behind the wheel.

"Fine," she snapped, snatching her keys back from my hand. "I'll drive. Jack, C'mon."

I watched her start to step down the stone staircase, Jack following happily. A glass beer bottle hung from his fingertips, almost half full. I didn't want them to get hurt, and Annie had even asked me to drive first. Maybe she thought she was too drunk *and trusted me to do it, and at that point, the overthought thoughts rolled in.*

"Wait," I called. Annie spun on her heel, and all I wanted was to get the annoyed look off her face. "I'll drive."

Jess squeezed my hand, pulling me back into the present, and grinned. She practically exuded excitement. "Ready?"

Chapter 11

We both entered through the door, the music streaming louder, if that were even possible. I didn't have time to linger on the anxiety I felt from buried memories intruding themselves on my life. The traffic of people near the door wasn't as heavy as I thought it'd be, but as we moved further into the party, down the hallway, and past the living room, the room was packed. My senses exploded, having trouble settling on just one.

It smelled like a mixture of beer and perfume, which, together, was not a perfect harmony. I wrinkled my nose. The level of noise wound a knot in my chest, tight and fixated. I scanned the heads for a blonde one. If Annie saw me there, it was over.

Indefinitely.

Someone bumped into me, their beer sloshing onto my bare arm. I glared at the girl, who didn't seem to know up from down at that point, as she made her way through the maze of Royal High's students.

"There's a lot of people here," I said to Jess, whose eyes were wide and lively. Jess always loved the party scene, but find me someone at Royal High who didn't. Oh, wait! Me.

"What?" she said back, the music drowning any hope of conversation. I shrugged, forgetting it and checking my phone time. We'd only been there for four minutes, and I was planning on being here for another four before ditching.

Technically, I wouldn't have lied to my parents, right? I said

I was going to Eric's party, but not for how long. I smiled to myself, content for just a moment in the sea of teenage absurdity. Penny Brooks: Queen of loopholes. "Jess!" Her head shot up toward the kitchen, grinning. Miles, from Jess and I's fifth period, waved at her. He was grinning sloppily from ear to ear, his secret crush on her quickly becoming less of a secret.

I looked at her, expecting her to either stay by my side or bring me with her. But she just rolled her eyes, smiling and leaning close. "I'm getting a drink. I'll be right back." She was gone before I could answer, leaving me standing alone in the mass of people.

I looked around me, alarmed and feeling like prey. People weren't actually looking at me yet, but they would be soon. The alcohol was surely slowing the process of realization.

The song changed to heavy rap, sparking a new current of movement through the room. Guys and girls slipped past me, their arms brushing against my own. A familiar tightening started in my belly, making its way up my chest. I tried to reach for my hair, but it was brushed to the side, and there were too many people around me to fix it. A heat swept over my body.

I searched for Jess, finally spotting her at the other end of the room. She was pressed against the pantry door, a drink in her hand and a flirty smile to match it. Miles's figure towered over her, but there may have been exactly four inches of space between the two of them.

Great. Thanks for nothing, Jess.

I had to get out of there. My wingwoman already ditched me. I checked my time; fifteen minutes had passed. I turned. Jess could get a ride with Miles. I dodged around people, and I quickly realized that it was harder to get out than in. The party seemed to have doubled by the time Jess and I arrived, which deepened the tightening in my chest. If Annie wasn't here yet, she'd be at any moment. She was a stickler for showing up fashionably late.

The front door opened, revealing a rush of incomers. Among those, a platinum blonde head stood out.

A breath hitched in my throat, and I had to think fast. I spotted a bathroom a few feet in front of me, so I shoved past people as quickly as I could. I didn't care if I was causing too much attention to myself; anything was better than being spotted by her.

I finally reached the handle, pulling and stumbling into the four-by-four bathroom. I pulled it shut, locking it and sighing a breath against my racing heart. I figured I could wait a few moments for Annie to make her way to the beer pong, then make my escape.

"Uh, hey," a deep voice said behind me.

I yelped, spinning and slamming back into the door. Hampton was standing in front of the toilet, peeing.

"Oh my god," I slapped a hand over my eyes. "Oh my god."

He answered with an awkward laugh, the sound of his stream sounding loudly against the toilet. "Must've forgot to lock the door."

"I'm so sorry," I said, my heart returning to its racing pace.

"It's my fault." We stayed in silence, or as much silence as there could be while he urinated four feet from me.

"This is awkward."

I laughed nervously, my hand still covering my eyes. Finally, it stopped, and the sound of his zipper finished it off.

"You can take your hands away now," he said.

I blinked against the new lighting. He was at the sink, washing his hands. His broad back faced me, and I realized just then how tall he was. Probably a good six inches taller than me.

"Um, not to be rude"—he cleared his throat and looked at me in the mirror—"but why are you still here?"

"I…" My lips parted, but nothing followed. He waited, still washing his hands. A smile tugged at the corner of his lips.

"Are you drunk?" he asked lazily, smiling to himself and drying his hands.

"No," I said quickly. Evenly. "I just… had to get away from someone."

Hampton nodded, turning off the sink and drying his hands on a towel. "Fight with a boyfriend?" *You have no idea.*

I literally laughed; it sounded sarcastic and forced. "No." I wasn't even sure if Justin was there, but he might've been.

"Friend, then?"

More like a slow-burning fight with one victorious side and another barely raising a tattered, white flag. That's me. I'm the white flag.

I managed a nod, only about a foot away from him. "Want me to help keep watch?"

My chest warmed. Sweet. But I shook my head, checking the time. "That's okay." Twenty-five minutes, then. How had it almost been thirty minutes when I was only planning on staying much less?

"You sure?"

I nodded, very sure.

He looked down at his hands and back at me. "We haven't really talked since you were my tour guide. You kinda ditched me."

My lips parted in response, speechless.

He shrugged somberly, looking at his feet. "It's okay, though. I have to get used to people not always liking me."

I found myself rushing to correct what I'd made him think.

"No, it's not that—"

"Then what is it?" He stepped closer, closing the gap between us. I swallowed. "Sometimes I can freak people out because I'm so extroverted. My brother told me that once." I shook my head, wanting him to continue. With what, I wasn't sure.

A step closer. I could smell him. Clean laundry. A faint, expensive-smelling spritz of cologne. A hint of beer.

"Did I freak you out?" he asked, genuinely glimpsing at me through his long, silky eyelashes.

"No," I whispered. I wanted him to come closer. He didn't, but he was so close that I could feel his body heat.

"I've been looking for you," he said quietly. "But you're pretty good at not being seen."

"I try." I gave a tiny smile, glancing at his lips. He caught me, surprise dawning over his eyes. Did I *really* just look at his lips? *Time to get a grip, Penny.*

I straightened. "How's it all been? Are you fitting in?"

He watched me for a moment, waiting for a beat to respond and reach my level of platonism.

"It's been good. Everyone's been super nice, so I can't complain. I like it here."

"Royal High or this town?"

"Both," he said, leaning against the wall connecting to the door. I must've made a face because he gave out a vibrant laugh, one so contagious it lingered. I could tell why people were drawn to him; here we were, standing in a house party bathroom, but it hardly felt like it.

"Why?" he asked. "You don't like it?"

"It's home." I shrugged. "So, I guess I'll always like it, but..." His gaze made me feel calm, so I said, "It hasn't felt that way recently."

Hampton gave a slow nod. "Sounds like a conversation for another time. Maybe one that's not in a bathroom?"

A newly born butterfly or two flitted around my tummy. My heart hammered, and right when my lips parted, the door to the bathroom flew open.

Chapter 12

We both jumped, the once-muffled music now blasting through the open door.

"Oh, sorry." Aaron Blackford, a senior who I've known since seventh-grade biology, stopped. His drunken gaze settled on my face, realization slowly sweeping over his own.

"Party-Penny! I haven't seen you at one of these since—"

I rushed forward, brushing past him and into the hallway. It was even stuffier than before, with people milling around and laughing at things that probably weren't even that funny.

The butterflies were gone, released into the loud room to find some other vulnerable girl. I had to get out of there. People started to notice the commotion, the bathroom light cutting the dimness in the hallway.

A hand rested on my bare shoulder. I whipped around, finding Hampton. He searched my face, his hand still on my shoulder. "Are you okay?"

I wanted to answer, "No. I'm not okay; I'm having raging anxiety that I can't seem to shake," but at the risk of sounding unhinged, I didn't. Instead, I gave a quick nod. I couldn't waste any more time. Annie would find me soon.

"Penny?" Justin suddenly emerged from the crowd. He looked at Hampton's hand on my shoulder, his expression turning hard.

"Justin, hey." Hampton took his hand away, dabbing him up. *So, they were friends.* But Justin's gaze was glued on me. I dropped my head.

"What are you doing here?" Justin asked, looking genuinely interested in my answer. Or hoping to catch me in a lie.

"I came with Jess." Jess was nowhere to be found, so that didn't help my case. He only nodded, accepting it.

"Here." Hampton put up a finger, stopping a girl who was passing us. He said something in her ear, her face turning bright pink—it was even visible in the darkness. He pointed to her glass, where she nodded quickly and handed him her drink. She headed back to the kitchen. *So, what? He's asking girls for their drinks now?*

"Take this." The solo cup was handed to me.

"I don't—"

"She doesn't—" Justin and I started at the same time, with Hampton looking between the two of us.

"I don't drink," I said.

He shrugged. "Take it anyway. You'll look less vulnerable."

Justin bit his lip, and I could tell it was killing him. What 'it' was, I wasn't so sure.

Hampton and I held each other's eyes like he was tempting me to cross a line I had set for myself. Or a line set by Royal High. I took the drink, holding it a few inches from my chest. I nodded a thank you, and he returned the nod.

"What the hell are you doing here?" Annie stepped between us. The mosh pit of my story's main characters nearly gave me whiplash.

"Annie, back off." Justin made an attempt to save me but, as usual, had nothing against Annie. Even when we'd been dating, he was no match for her.

She stepped closer to me. "Makes sense you decided to come here. Of all places."

I swallowed, looking her dead in the eye.

She eyed the drink in my hand, giving a short laugh. "Feeling homesick, Penny?" Before I could even think of a response, she slapped the cup out of my hand. It fell to the ground, silenced by the banging music. The mysterious liquid sloshed around my feet. "You won't need that. Alcohol and you don't go over so well, remember?"

Hampton suddenly stepped around her, whispering in her ear. The two of them together—they looked perfect. **It made sense she'd already managed to sink her claws into him.** He pulled away, and her bitch-face half melted away. What was left was just her normal bitch-face, probably only detectable to me.

Hampton looked at me, tipping his head away from the fiasco. I gladly agreed, leaving Justin and Annie without a second glance. I finally made it to the door, the crowd of people somehow less stuffy than before, and let myself into the salty night air.

I breathed in deeply, happy to have my personal space back. The door clicked shut behind me, and I half-expectantly turned to see Annie following me. But it wasn't Annie; it was Hampton.

"What are you doing?"

He raised his eyebrows, pointing back toward the house. "Following you."

"Why?"

"Because I saved you from a wrestling match." He said it like it was obvious. So many questions.

"I was handling it fine just on my own, thanks."

Hampton readjusted his long-sleeved pullover, smirking. "Well, it didn't seem like Justin was gonna jump in any time soon." Was that a hint of jealousy I detected? One of my butterflies attempted to return, but I swatted it away.

Justin always tried to help. But it wasn't his job any more. And it certainly wasn't Hampton's. I hopped down the steps, watching my fellow intoxicated classmates pass me to enter the party.

"No, 'thank you'?" he called. Silence was his answer, but that didn't stop him. "Do you need a ride somewhere?"

I froze, turning. "You've been drinking."

He raised an eyebrow, surprised that that was what it took to get me to acknowledge him. "Barely. I've had, like, three beers."

My throat dried. "You really shouldn't drive when you've been drinking." His eyebrows, hitched together, softened.

"You're right," he said. "I'm sorry." I studied his face. He meant it.

I spun back around, making my way toward Jess's car. "Not to be rude," I started, my tone of voice most definitely suggesting otherwise, "but why are you so inclined to help me?"

"We both said, 'not to be rude,' tonight." I smiled a tiny smile to myself, reaching her car.

"Isn't that interesting?"

I turned to him, making a face. "Isn't *what* interesting?"

He had a reminiscent look on his face. "I don't know, like how when someone is about to say something even remotely rude, they start it with 'not to be rude', just so they have free will to say whatever the hell they want?" He shrugged. "It's kinda bullshit."

"A lot of things are bullshit," I said.

He frowned. "True. But a lot of things are beautiful. Depends how you look at it."

Suddenly, very aware of my own voice amidst the Port Royal silence, I said, "I think I'm gonna go." I reached on top of the front wheel, snatching her keys.

"Well, I can't go back in there now," he started, his tone the same as it was the day he pleaded with me outside of school when I was suddenly the only person who could give him the tour.

"Why?"

"Because I told Annie I'd be her partner in a game of pong. You know, to save you."

"You better get going, then. Annie doesn't like to wait long."

"You seem to know a lot about Annie," he said.

"Were you best friends once upon a time?" I shrugged, feigning to be bored of the conversation when, really, the tiniest part of me begged him to continue.

"Oh, I get it," Hampton said, leaning against Jess car and facing me.

"She's mad at you for something you actually didn't do, but she thinks you did, and she's turned everyone against you." I stared, fear trickling through me. Someone told him, and that's why he wants to get close to me. *I'm his trauma porn.*

But he grinned victoriously, and I relaxed. No one would be smiling over a dead eighteen-year-old. "I *knew* it was over, some guy. So, what? She thinks you stole her boyfriend? Or," he leaned in closer, "did you *actually* steal her boyfriend? Because then I would have to seriously consider changing sides."

I lightly shoved his shoulder. "No, stupid. I'm going home now. Enjoy your beer pong."

Hampton shook his head, rolling his green eyes. "I'd rather have an excuse to not be," he paused, a shift in his tone, "and you seem like a pretty good excuse."

"Oh." I nodded. "What every girl wants to hear." My quick comeback startled me, and it was at that moment that I realized it was Hampton who helped me... *forget.*

Temporarily, at least. But still. I shifted, uncomfortable with the sudden realization. I was getting too attached; I could feel it. My strong edges were softening. Blurring. Reaching out to Hampton's voice. Annie would never allow it. No one would allow it.

"I didn't mean it like that," he said, "just that I'd rather hang with you than Annie in some stupid game of beer bong."

He looked around, looking to make sure the coast was clear. "Wanna know a secret?" I raised an eyebrow just when he dropped to a whisper, "I don't even like beer."

"That's your secret?"

"Beer pong is my worst nightmare. Don't even get me started on the flip cup."

I rolled my eyes. If only he knew my secrets, they'd blow him out of the water.

"You don't seem very satisfied with my confession."

"Confession?" I laughed. Hampton nodded, amusement tugging on his lips. "That's not a very good secret."

He put a hand to his heart, tilting his head. "That hurt." I forced my mouth to stay in a disinterested line when it screamed at me to pull upward.

Hampton stepped closer, the mood shifting. "If you're such an expert, try me." I didn't answer, searching for a more legitimate question. He took another tiny step. "Got any secrets?"

My lips parted, suddenly dry. My heart hammered hard in my chest, and I whispered, "No."

He squinted his eyes. "I don't believe you."

I shrugged, my mouth more than happy to stay in a frown at that time.

"Fine, fine." He laughed, holding up a hand in the air as if pledging, "I, Hampton Prescott, promise to tell you a better secret. At some point." I managed a half-smile.

"Deal?" He held out a hand, waiting for me to shake it.

I eyed it, putting my hand in his. "Deal."

"Hampton! Dude!" Aaron yelled from the front door. Both our heads snapped to the voice, and by reflex, I immediately separated myself from him. I back-stepped into the dark, realizing how close we'd been.

"What?"

"We're waiting on you for the next round."

Hampton looked at me with a semi-tortured look, but I was already getting in my car. I'd been there for almost an hour, and my usual cafe was still open. *Chai latte, here I come.*

"You're leaving," he said. A sad note lingered in his voice.

I ducked into the car, settling into the driver's seat. "Go play."

"Hampton!" Aaron yelled again. I shut the door, severing the connection between us. Jess hadn't texted me, and I wasn't even sure if she realized I was gone. I figured she could get a ride from Miles. I flicked on my lights, waiting for Hampton's figure to step away before pulling out and heading to my latte.

Chapter 13

I woke to hard knocks against my bedroom door. I opened my eyes, groaning and flipping to my stomach.

"Good morning, sunshine." Dad's voice interrupted the sweet, sweet silence of the room. "Pancakes downstairs. Bacon. Eggs. Coffee."

"I hate coffee," I said into the pillow, voice muffled. He sat on the edge of my bed, the mattress dipping.

"We also have orange juice," he said with a sigh. Dad loved coffee. "How was the party last night? We were asleep by the time you got back."

I rolled over, raising a suspicious eyebrow. "Did Mom send you up here to ask?"

He shook his head. "Nope. Dad's honor. Thought I'd get the inside scoop before she asks."

I smiled a tired smile. What he really meant was, "Thought I'd ask you peacefully before Mom brought out the knives." Okay, I was being dramatic. But I wouldn't put it past her.

I thought of Hampton and our banter. And then, of how close he was to me in the bathroom, his smell invading my senses, my eyes lingering on his lips—Dad gave me a tilt of his head, smiling.

"Looks like it went well!" He draped the dish towel over his left shoulder. "Did you see Annie there?" I thought back to her aggressive gaze and the way she slapped the drink out of my hand.

"Noted," Dad said, raising an eyebrow at the quick shift in my facial expression.

I turned my head to the window, looking at my favorite tree. The morning sunshine danced over the leaves. I never told them specifics about Annie and I, just that we weren't friends any more. And that our friendship took a gentle nosedive, sparing them the crashing and burning details. They didn't press it and probably assumed it was too painful for me to talk about, in addition to the night of Eric's party—the last one, I mean.

He seemed to get it, patting my leg and standing. "Come down before everything gets cold. You know how my pancakes are only good when they're warm."

"Your pancakes are good, hot or cold, and you know it."

"Oh, I know," he said, starting to shut the door. "Just wanted to hear you say it." I rolled my eyes, getting out of bed and crossing the room to the door. By the time I got downstairs, still in pjs and hair still frizzy, I began piling my plate. Two pancakes because I was planning on getting two more, bacon and scrambled eggs. My parents adopted the breakfast tradition a few months back, most likely something Dr. Yao suggested. Something about food having the power to bring us together, blah, blah, blah. But to be fair, a tiny part of me looked forward to Dad's buttery pancakes every Saturday.

"Morning, sweetie," Mom said from the table, sipping her coffee. She looked immaculate because, of course, she was on a Saturday morning with nowhere to go. I poured my frustration in syrup form over my plate, watching it pool over the pancakes and settle on the plate. I moved to the table.

"Morning."

"Dad said the party was good last night?"

I nodded, cutting into the buttery pancake. I could feel her watching me, but I kept my eyes trained on the plate.

"Did you see—?" A knock at the front door interrupted her, thank God, and she jumped up with perkiness. I took a sip of my orange juice, freshly squeezed by Dad. I kept eating, with Dad squinting into his phone and reading some emails (he refused to accept the fact that his eyes were going on him).

Mom walked back into the kitchen, looking more excited than when she left the table.

I resisted the urge to roll my eyes. "What?"

"It's for you."

Jess. I woke up to texts from her but didn't have the energy to answer yet. True—I stole her car and kinda left her in the dust. So, I had a bit of apologizing on my end, too. I ended up parking her car in her driveway and walking the rest of the way home, which isn't a big deal. A mile or so at most. I stood, bringing my plate with me to the door. Maybe I could offer some of my food as a peace offering for leaving her. To my defense, she left me, too. And I was still a little mad. I ate another piece of my pancake on the way through the kitchen. **She must've felt pretty bad to have sacrificed her precious morning sleep.** I decided on my short walk to let it go, spearing a piece on my fork and planning on giving her a sneak peek of my offering.

I reached the foyer, grabbed the door and pulled it open. My arm shot out with the fork, ready to hear her laugh, but froze.

Hampton Prescott stood on my porch. On my porch, blinking at the piece of pancake in his face. "Oh my god," I pulling the fork back and dropping it on my plate. It was covered in syrup, no doubt, but my only concern was the school's celebrity standing in front of me.

"This looks weird, I know. Well, now that I'm actually standing here on your porch, I'm realizing how weird this is."

I glanced at my pjs and the grip I had on my plate of food. I didn't even want to think about my hair. Or the acne treatment leftover from last night. My face burned. "What are you doing here?"

"I just wanted to see if you were okay from…" He trailed off, searching for words. "From last night."

I nodded, speechless.

"Good." He nodded.

"You came all the way here to ask me if I'm okay?"

"I thought it'd mean more than a text." He shrugged. "Plus, those kinds of things make it seem like I'm hitting on you or something."

The old me would have taken this golden moment to flirt, asking him something like, "Aren't you?"

But instead, I raised an eyebrow and paraphrased, "What do you call this?"

Hampton gave me a smile, putting out his hand like he did last night. "The start of a friendship. I told you we were going to be friends, eventually."

"Did you?"

"In some form or another." I plucked a piece of bacon off my plate and ate it, mostly because I was already so low on the humiliation scale—it couldn't get any worse. Might as well embrace it.

"This is eventually."

I chewed slowly, trying to look like I was deliberating the friendship. Okay, half of me was telling me to slam the door and go back to my room, away from the world and judging eyes. But the other half… the other half told me that Hampton might be a good excuse for my parents to think I was moving on. For the threat of Dr. Yao's return and move to Arizona. For Mrs. Pricket's demands.

"You know a friendship is usually consensual," I said.

"Don't worry, I'm okay with it."

I laughed. You know, so my parents could hear. "Fine. We can be friends."

Hampton tugged at his sleeve, a small smile on his face. "I'm glad we've reached an understanding."

We stood in silence for a moment until I realized I was still in my pajamas, sporting a good bedhead, and holding a plate full of food. "I'll see you at school then."

I went to close the door, but he stepped forward and put a hand on it. "Wait, wait. We're friends now."

"I think we just acknowledged that."

He rolled his eyes. "Which means we'll have to do something. To start a friendship."

"I don't think that's how that works," I said, a laugh creeping into my tone.

"It does in New York."

I eyed him, wondering if that were true. Nerves swirled in my tummy. "Well, what do you want to do?"

"Already planned." He grinned, looking my outfit up and down. "You can come with me dressed like that if you really want, but…"

I gave him a look, telling him I'd be ready in a moment and to wait. I left him standing on the porch, crossing back into the kitchen and putting my plate on the counter.

"I'm going out," I announced, knowing my mom was happy and already rethinking Dr. Yao.

"With Hampton?" she asked, her tone tentative in trying hard to not expel exclamation points. She must've formerly met him at the door, finally putting a face to the tour guide I'd led.

I nodded, heading upstairs to change. *You know that stupid saying where it says that things are put in your life for a reason? A reason bigger than yourself?* I climbed the steps, smiling.

Finally, the world decided to give me a break. I was expected to move on and accept what happened, and I don't think I was ever capable of doing that, not after everything I did.

But Hampton was my living excuse. One with a heartbeat. I could pretend I was okay.

Chapter 14

I stepped up into his black Audi, settling into the seat and instantly second-guessing the entire thing. I glanced at Hampton, reminding myself that in order to stay in the clear with my parents, this was what had to be done. I needed to pretend to be a socialite again.

"Where to?" He joined me, getting in and buckling his seatbelt.

I just looked at him. "I thought you had a plan."

"Oh, I do." He put the car in reverse, pulling out of the driveway. "I just wanted to see if you had anything in mind."

I eyed the huge tree casting shadows on the house and over my window, part of me wishing I was in my room. In my bed. Away from Hampton and his weird jokes. "So, where are we going?"

"Well, we have two stops," he said, turning out of my driveway. "The first one is the farmer's market."

"I just ate," I said instinctively, almost like a reflex, because that's what you say, right? But it was true. Plus, the farmer's market was crawling with kids and their parents, especially their parents, on Saturdays. I didn't remember the last time I had been to the market. I never wanted to go with Mom any more, so she eventually stopped asking.

"That's okay. You'll be hungry later, right?" Jeez, he wasn't taking no for an answer. I stared out the window, watching the outside world pass by. Maybe he'd park far away, and I could stay in the car. That way, no one will see me.

I nodded, knowing I would be hungry and practically feeling my tummy preparing to grumble in an hour. He put down both driver's and passenger side windows, air streaming through and blowing my hair around. The familiar saltiness of the nearby water filled the car, and part of my anxiety was put to ease. As much as I hated Port Royal and everyone in it, I could never hate the smell.

Hampton put one hand on the steering wheel, dropping the other to his lap. "What's this place called again? My mom told me, but I forgot."

"Moe's." Moe's Farmer's Market was the next best thing next to the Creamy & Creamier Creamery. Moe's was Annie and my favorite spot on the weekends; we'd grab some fruit and head to the dock, gossiping the whole time and making fun of strangers as they passed.

Hampton glanced at me. "Do you go there a lot?" I contemplated the question. His tone.

A tiny voice whispered in my head, urging me to lie. It was what was best. He can't know. Not yet. "Yeah." I gave him a smile. "All the time."

"What's your favorite thing to get?"

I didn't even need to think about it. "Chocolate-covered potato chips."

He made a face, looking disgusted. "Penny."

I laughed at his face, wanting to defend Annie and my favorite snack. "They're so good. I'm surprised you haven't had them, being from New York and all."

"New York is more... *refined*." Despite my scoff, he continued, "I think my body is thanking me for not having them."

"Drama queen." I rolled my eyes.

"That's what you said when you met me." He looked at me, giving me a smile that pressed dimples into his cheeks.

"You have to try them," I said, crossing my legs.

He seemed to contemplate this, drumming his fingers against the wheel at the stop light. "Fine. But only if you promise me one thing."

I raised an eyebrow, waiting.

"You have to tell me one thing about yourself. At some point today."

Why would he care if I told him something about myself? He could find out plenty by asking anyone, but it seemed like no one had yet. "What do you want to know?"

"Anything you wanna tell me."

My hands unclenched. Anything; that was easy enough.

"All for a potato chip that's capable of changing your life?"

Hampton laughed, turning the wheel and pulling into the crowded gravel parking lot. "I don't think it'll be that good..." He trailed off, pulling into a free spot. He put the car in park and turned to me. "But I'm willing to try it."

I blinked, having been so lost in the conversation that I didn't even realize we were sitting near the entrance of Moe's. As predicted, most Port Royal residents milled around. Little kids ran and played tag in the grassy front of the shops, giggling.

"Deal," I said.

Hampton nodded, content, and pulled open his door. It was just a potato chip, and all he wanted to know was just one thing. It could be my favorite color. My favorite animal. My first grade teacher's name. But it felt like I promised him something bigger than that. The stirring feeling in my stomach told me I didn't like that.

*

"There's so much stuff here." His eyes scanned the multiple stands: baked goods, fresh fruits and veggies, bread, organic pieces of arts and crafts, handmade children's games, and candy literally reflected against the pool of his eyes—vibrantly green that day.

"Have you ever been to something like this?"

"Nothing to this extent," he said. "I mean, there's vendors in the streets. And I would sometimes go to farmer's markets in Connecticut when we visited my grandparents, but no. This is insane."

While Hampton stood there for another moment, surveying the wonders of Moe's, I did as well, but not in the way he was. I was scanning the crowd for a familiar blonde, her friends, or literally anyone from school.

"So, where are these potato chips?" His voice jarred me, pulling me back.

"Follow me." I tipped my head to the right. I led him through the maze of people, sidestepping older couples who were more interested in the baked brioche bread than the traffic around them.

We passed the stand of candy, smiling at the kids who stood and stared at the handcrafted jawbreakers and lollipops, and finally stopped at Ben's fudge stand.

Ben, an older man who had to be nearing his seventies, smiled a toothy grin once he saw me. "Penelope! I haven't seen you in forever!"

"Hi, Ben," I said, giving into the muscles that pulled my lips into a smile. He was my second favorite part of the Moe's. "How are you?"

Ben placed a crinkly hand on the wooden island, smiling. "Oh, good as always. How have you been, Sunshine?" He used to always call me Sunshine, but never Annie. I think it bothered her that she didn't get a special nickname like I did. I assured her it wasn't personal and that a nickname didn't mean anything. But I secretly knew he liked me more.

"I've been…" I searched for a word, never wanting to lie to Ben as I did with everyone else. But Hampton stood by my side, able to hear every word.

"Okay. Things are fine."

Ben nodded, seeming to get it. He knew what happened, but he seemed to be the only person who didn't judge me for it. "Who's your friend?"

"This is Hampton." I gestured. "He just transferred to Royal High."

Ben put a hand out, reaching over his homemade blocks of fudge. "Hello, Hampton. It's always nice to meet a friend of Penny's."

Hampton shook his hand. "It's nice to meet you too, sir."

"Well, if I know Penny, then she's here for chocolate-covered potato chips."

I grinned. "Yes, please."

Ben nodded, reaching behind him to the shelves. He plucked a bag, handing it over. I went to take out some cash, but he held up a hand. "No need. My treat."

I took the bag tentatively, frowning. "Are you sure?"

"Yes, yes." He shoed the matter away. "I'm just happy to see you again." We talked for a bit more about school, how my family was, and what colleges we were looking into until another customer visited his booth, and we said our goodbyes.

"He's awesome," he said when we walked away.

I nodded, holding the delicately wrapped bag in my hand. The twine used to tie it shut flowed down a few inches. "Yeah, he's pretty cool."

"All right, I think I saw sandwiches back there. What do you want?" Sandwiches?

How long was this day going to be?

"Ham?" I said it like a question, but he nodded, and I followed him to the booth. He ordered a ham sandwich as well as a salami with mustard. He paid, thanking the woman who handed him the paper bag with freshly made deli sandwiches. A step over, we browsed the fruits and chose peaches and blueberries. "Ready?" We were holding two bags brimming with food, and he held up a finger.

"One sec, stay here." He jogged off before I could answer. I was left alone, the familiar anxiety settling in the pit of my stomach. I tried to focus my attention on the traffic of people—the happy and laughing children and adults when I met eyes with Mrs. Doe.

The same Mrs. Doe that was Jack's mom. The same Mom I met eyes with in the pitch-darkness of the night, pierced only by flashing red and blue lights.

That night, they were streaked with tears and anguish.

That day, in the middle of Moe's, she gave me a deep, hollow stare.

My body flushed with more chills than I could handle, not knowing what to do. I felt seized and choked, a foreign and invisible hand gripping my throat and refusing to release. Mrs. Doe's mouth went into a straight line, so straight that it looked as if she were using all the strength in her body to force her lips shut and not make a scene.

"Ready?" Hampton appeared back into the scene, blocking

her from my vision and holding out a paper-wrapped bundle of orange daisies.

The harsh shift startled me, and I let out a jagged breath. My shoulders rose and fell fast, begging for air.

"Are you okay?" His voice softened.

I peered around him, but Mrs. Doe had already left. "Penny?" he repeated.

I looked him in the eyes, managing a nod.

Hampton didn't seem too convinced; he blinked once or twice more before handing the flowers to me, giving me a tentative smile. "For you. I hope you like daisies."

Chapter 15

The car ride was quiet. I sat in the passenger's seat, a bouquet of daisies lying on my lap as I stared out the window. Port Royal whizzed by, with the sun shining high in the sky and kids running to the beach to try and get some tanning before the cold set in. November would be there soon, with the familiar bite of chill that would surely come.

"So, about last night," he started, and I tensed, no idea what he was about to say, "do you hide in bathrooms often, or was that just a one-time thing?"

I smiled, careful with my words. "I actually haven't been going to the parties lately."

"Really?" he asked. "You seemed to be the life of the party last night." I swatted his arm, and he exclaimed, "Hey, hey! I'm driving here."

I jumped to change the subject. "What were the parties like in New York?" That time, it was he who paused to consider his words.

"Nothing major like you'd think," he said. "I mostly stayed in my friend group from school."

"What was your school like?"

He pulled into the sandy parking lot. "Different." I looked at him.

"Different, how?"

"Geez, if I knew you were going to talk this much, I never would have picked you up." The car jolted a bit, switching to park. "Ready to picnic?"

I peered at Hampton, his back toward me as he climbed out of the car. Was Hampton keeping as many secrets as me? I sat for a moment, shaking my head. I doubt Hampton was capable of doing something as messed up as me.

I opened my door, stepping onto the gravel and sand. The crunch of both Hampton and I's feet were comforting, filling the air around us and competing with the noise of the shore's waves lapping against the sand. He pulled out the bag of food, and I followed him to where the gravel met the sand.

"Do you want to walk and eat or sit?" He looked over at me, holding up the bag of goods. I took a quick glance at our surroundings, knowing it would look worse if someone saw Port Royal's newcomer having a sit-down lunch with the most hated.

"Walk?" I suggested, and we started down the beach. He pulled my sandwich out of the bag, handing it to me. I unwrapped the paper, took a bite, and looked out over the water. He was the answer, Penny. The answer to getting my parents off my ass.

"Do you miss New York?" I asked. It's not like I cared, really. I just wanted to alleviate the silence. We bent down to untie our shoes, slipping them off and dangling them in our hands.

"Yeah," he said, "I do. I grew up with all my friends there, so mostly it's them I miss." I nodded along like I understood, but really, I didn't. I'd never moved, but I *had* lost all my friends. I shook my head, reminding myself that it wasn't the same.

I took a bite, munching and swallowing before saying, "It must be hard to leave senior year." I looked at him, curious to see his reaction. He didn't say anything for a good beat, a blank expression on his face. So, he and his family just packed up and left. Hardly. My curiosity tipped me further down the path of questioning, and I couldn't help myself.

"You said you had a brother?" I asked. I didn't know why, but I half-expected him to have lied. That I would catch him at that moment, but he smiled instantly.

"Little brother," he replied almost instantly. "He's nine." God, Penny. Had I become such a pathological liar that I couldn't possibly imagine anyone else to be truthful? I jutted out my lower lip, imagining how cute a nine-year-old version of Hampton would be. I stopped mid-step, surprising myself with the thought. I looked out over the water, wondering if the seawater was getting to me. Or Jess. I had to stop listening to her rants about Hampton's hotness factor.

"He's pretty excited about the move. Loves that a beach is in his backyard." He took another bite of his sandwich, a breeze tousling his dirty blond hair.

"I didn't know you had a brother. Or, did I?"

"It's crazy what you find out about someone when you have a conversation," he said with a smile in his tone.

I looked at him, smiling. "Fair point." We continued our walk for a few moments in silence, the water creeping up the sand every few seconds. The coldness trickled over our bare feet. "What's your brother's name?"

"Jayden."

"Cute name," I said, handing my trash to his outstretched hand. "Is he anything like you?"

"By that, if you mean funny, talented, and charming, then yes." He smiled, a smile that revealed dimples. "He is."

"You're not that funny," I mused. That time, he gave me a light shove.

"No, he actually isn't at all like me," he said, his tone growing serious. "Um, he has something called PDD. Stands for

Pervasive Development Disorder." I wasn't sure what he was going to say, but it sure wasn't that. "Just a fancy way of saying he has a delay in socializing or communication skills. We noticed it when he was around two or three years old. It's a type of autism, so he's on the spectrum."

I stopped walking, turning to him. "I'm sorry. I didn't know."

He gave a half-smile. "It's okay—he's still pretty awesome. He's smart, like really smart, in science and stuff. Something *definitely* not like me. I'm more of a history guy myself."

"Well, I hope to meet him." I said it so quickly that I wanted to clamp my hand over my mouth. How could that have leaked out so easily? I had once been a flirtatious enough person to know what flirting sounded like, and that was it. I was practically inviting myself over to his house.

"Me too," he said, fishing out the bag of chocolate-covered potato chips. "These better be the best thing I've ever eaten, or we can no longer be friends."

I plucked the bag from his hand, untwisting the top. "Who said we were friends?"

"So you bring people you're not friends with to the beach?"

I got the bag open, tilting my head at him. "I'm pretty sure you showed up at my house."

"Right, right." He held up his hands in surrender, smiling at the ground. "I'm ready to try it." He reached into the bag, pulling one out and clinking it to mine like we were taking shots. We popped them in our mouths, and I watched him chew.

"So?" I prompted. He nodded slowly, giving a little cough.

"Actually," he said, clearing his throat. "Really good."

"You want another?" I held the bag out, but he shook his head and put a hand to his stomach. "I'm so full. Maybe later?"

I was instantly thrown from the beach with Hampton into the recurring memory.

"Maybe we should do this later?" Jack and Annie stepped down the steps to Eric's house; Annie's walk was miraculously stable for someone who had been drinking for hours on heels. Jack, in a polar opposite fashion, walked without poise and swayed harshly. His arm remained snug around Annie's waist. Watching Jack's drunken state sent warning signs through my brain, interrupting my own drunken haze.

"Penny, stop being such a PB&J," Annie said, and it felt like she had slapped me.

Being called a PB&J was the worst I could've stooped. My stomach burned; I didn't want her to be upset with me.

Jack reached for the door, pulling the handle. It remained locked, and he pouted. "Party-Penny! Open the door! Chicken nuggets await me." I eyed the keys in my hand. It was pretty late. No one would be out right now.

How hard could it be to drive? Plus, it looked like Jack needed food ASAP.

Annie groaned loudly. "Can you, for once, take a risk? God, you can be so boring sometimes." She turned to Jack, running a hand through his hair.

He smiled a goofy smile. "That feels good." It wasn't that far. Just a few blocks. I think Justin had done it before, too, and that's when I got the grand idea:

"Should I get Justin to bring us? I don't think he's been drinking too much." I smiled, relieved that I had gotten out of doing something stupid. I started to move around the car. "I'll go get him right now."

"There she goes again," Annie mumbled in a not-so-quiet voice to Justin.

I stopped, the sudden movement jarring me a bit. My head swayed, feeling hurt.

"What do you mean?"

"Why does Justin always have to tag along? Why can't you just do something with your best friend?"

"And me." Jack held up a hand, leaning on the window of the car. "Don't forget about me." Annie ignored him, staring me dead in the eye.

"Just you and me. C'mon." Her eyes sparkled. "It'll be something everyone finds out about tomorrow." She fanned her hands, painting an invisible picture: "'Annie and Penny left Eric's lame party and drove when they weren't exactly sober.' If you thought people looked up to us now..." She shook her head, grinning. "You don't even know what's coming."

I looked between the house and Annie, feeling like I was teetering on the edge of a cliff. That's always how Annie made me feel, like I was on the edge of something dangerous, scary, and potentially spectacular.

"Fine," I said, returning to the car door. Jack made whooping sounds, throwing his arms in the air.

"Penny, you're the coolest," he said, jumping into the then-unlocked back seat.

Annie gave me an 'I told you so' look over the car, ducking her head into the passenger seat. I took a breath, got in, and started the ignition.

"Penny?" Hampton waved a hand in front of my face, and it was then that I realized I'd stopped walking. He stood in front of me, concern written across his slowly tanning skin.

"What?"

"I don't know," he said, blinking. "You just went somewhere."

I pressed my lips together, embarrassed. Had I really just done that in front of him? He was probably ready to cut and run at that very moment. "Sorry. I just thought of something. Something stupid."

He nodded, seeming unconvinced, but didn't press it. We continued on a walk; the only sound between us was the lapping of soft waves and the squawks of seagulls. And Hampton's occasional clearing of his throat. And coughs. And was that choking I heard?

"Are you okay?" I asked after the sixth cough.

"Yeah." He shooed it away. "Totally fine." I nodded.

"Is that…?" Hampton started, suddenly throwing up a hand and grinning.

"Hey, man!" I followed his gaze, finding Justin to be standing next to his mound of fishing gear. Justin was a big fisher; he always tried to make me come with him, telling me it'd be so romantic, but the truth was that I just didn't like seeing fish being sliced with the hook, even if it was temporary. Plus, what was so romantic about fish?

Justin stood from his fishing box, a tangle of wire in his hand. His eyes flickered between the two of us, and I could have only imagined what was going through his head. But Justin walked over to us both, playing every part of the chill ex-boyfriend who could care less if the new guy was walking on the beach with his ex-girlfriend. But I knew him; he cared. A lot. He just would never show it.

"Hey, dude," he greeted Hampton, turning and giving me a quick smile.

"Hi, Penny." I might've said hello back, and if I did, I couldn't hear myself over my pounding heartbeat. Was Justin going to run back to everyone at school and tell them about

Hampton and me?

"What're you guys doing?" Justin asked, shoving his hands into the pockets of his blue and green-rimmed swim shorts. Swim shorts that I bought him last Christmas. I tried not to stare at them.

"Just went for a walk," I said in an easy tone, but what sounded easy to me probably sounded awkward and forced to someone else. That was how it went, right?

Justin nodded in return, his eye lingering on mine for a moment before nodding to Hampton. "Perfect timing that I'm seeing you, actually. We're having a bonfire tonight, and everyone wants you to come. You in?" The bonfire. It was around that time when, a year prior, I was a part of the Mets, Justin by my side, and walking around with all the confidence in the world. It was crazy what a year could do. I tucked back a strand of hair, feeling awkward for not getting an invitation. I remember Annie got so drunk that I had to hold her hair back while she threw up in the bushes.

Hampton's face lit up. "Yeah, that sounds awesome." And then he turned to me, holding out a hand.

"Penny, you in?"

Me? What? Pretty sure I wasn't the one everyone wanted to come. I was more than pretty sure, actually. I was certain.

"Oh, um," I started, racking my brain to try and figure out a quick excuse. With both of them staring at me, my mind went blank.

"That's okay." Justin raised an eyebrow, bored and unsurprised. Justin wasn't ever a part of the Port Royal Hate Committee, and constantly urged me to try and get out there again. I remember being upset with him for not understanding that I just wasn't welcome any more.

"C'mon! It'll be fun," Hampton said.

"Penny doesn't go to parties," Justin cut in. "Not her scene." I looked at him, wanting so much to push him into the water, preferably near the taut fishing line.

Before anyone could answer, and just so I could wipe the cool-guy look off my ex's face, I slapped a smile on and said, "I'll be there."

*

"Who are you, and what have you done with my best friend?" Jess asked, crossing her arms and staring at me in shock. I lay on my bed, both arms crossed over my face. I didn't have an answer for her; *I* wasn't even sure. Jess showed up at the house after Hampton dropped me off, and we'd carried on like nothing had happened the night before.

"What have I done?" I mumbled through my arms.

"Savagery! That's what you've done!" Jess rubbed her palms together. "You're walking into a shark tank tonight with the most popular fish in the sea."

I dropped my arms, smiling. "Ms. Sing would be proud of your use of metaphors."

She held up a finger. "Actually, Ms. Sing said that the most obvious metaphors aren't actually metaphors at all. They're overused."

"Maybe you should become a writer," I said.

"Too much effort. Plus, I'm definitely not imaginative enough. Or sad." I laughed.

"Who said writers are sad?"

"Charlotte Brontë? Oscar Wilde?"

I stared at her. "What English classes are you taking?"

She shrugged, crossing the room to my bed, joining me but still in her own world. She'd flat-ironed her hair that morning, looking shinier and reaching her waistline. "I wish I could see the look on Annie's face."

"Are you sure you can't come?" I whined, sitting up and giving puppy-dog eyes.

Jess rolled her eyes. "You know how much shit I'd get for missing my brother's recital. My parents would freak." It was true. Her parents would really support one another when it was needed most, especially their achievements. Since Jess's family was artistically blessed, there was almost always something going on. Jess herself was an artist, her dad was an architect; her mom was a home designer; and her brother was a crazy good pianist.

I found myself shaking my head. "I can't go."

"Why?" She looked at me like I was crazy. "This is your moment to say," she jabbed both her middle fingers in my direction, "to all of them."

"What do I have that they don't have?" I sat back against my pillows.

"Hampton," she said slowly. "Duh."

"I don't," I threw up quotation marks with my index and middle finger, 'have' him."

"Hm, let's see." She looks up, tapping her finger to her chin.

"He showed up to your *house*, basically asked you on a date, bought food with you, and then went walking on the beach."

Well, when she put in like that.

"I just don't know why... I mean, it's pretty obvious that everyone hates me. And he's been hanging around Annie."

Jess patted her heart. "The heart wants what it wants."

I grabbed a pillow, throwing it at her. "Seriously! Why would he be into that?"

"You don't give yourself enough credit." Her grin slipped and was replaced with a half-smile.

"Just because you're not at the top anymore doesn't mean you've lost the person you are." It was her turn to throw the pillow at me.

"Don't you remember the girl that every guy was after?"

No, I didn't. "I had a boyfriend." Jess threw me a look. "Like that stopped them." She smiled.

"Don't sell yourself short here."

"Besides," she tossed her straight hair over her shoulder.

"Even if I'm not part of the Mets, I've still got it." We giggled.

I repositioned. "Speaking of. What happened last night? With Miles?"

Jess frowned. "I'm sorry about ditching you. I was pulled into things, and I totally forgot, and that makes me such a bad friend."

"Woah!" I let out a short laugh.

"I wasn't accusing you. I was just asking what happened with him." I wasn't mad at her any more; I knew she had the right to live her own life, and who was I to hold her back?

She nodded, shrugging. "Nothing, really. We made out for a little, and then that was it." I eyed her suspiciously, and she hit me.

"Seriously! I wasn't in the mood to go any further. Besides," a pause, "by the time I'd realized that you weren't there, I felt like shit."

"It's okay," I said, shrugging and thinking of my encounter with Hampton. "I was with Hampton."

Jess's jaw dropped as she jumped up from the bed. "What do you mean you were *with* Hampton?"

I laughed, not able to help it. "Not like that! We were in the bathroom."

"The *bathroom*?" she practically shrieked, doing tiny hops

of excitement.

"I walked in on him by accident, and we got to talking," I said, shaking my head.

"I swear. Nothing happened." She looked at me for a bit, eventually nodding and sitting back down.

"Well, you know what this means, right?"

I gave her a look, not knowing what it meant.

"It means that I'm getting you ready for tonight." She leaned closer. "And you're gonna walk in there like the boss-ass-bitch I know you are."

Chapter 16

Feeling nervous was an understatement. I made Jess pull over twice because I thought I was going to throw up.

"Why didn't you let him drive you again?" she asked, flicking her blinker on.

I held my stomach, putting the window down and letting the breeze hit me in the face. "Element of surprise." The window rolled back up.

"I'm not letting you mess up what I worked on for hours," she said.

"Fix your hair." I huffed, looking at myself in the mirror. Sparkly eyeshadow accented my eyes, along with the brush of blush, bronzer, and coat of foundation Jess had applied. I fixed a strand of my hair, which Jess had curled with slight beachy waves through it. I shifted in the seat, unable to keep still. I was comfy, dressed in ripped jean shorts and a light blue hoodie.

"Pull over," I said, feeling bile rise in my throat.

"You're fine," she deadpanned.

"We're almost there."

I swallowed the rising vomit. "It's your fault if I throw up in your car."

"God, I'm having such fomo." Fear of missing out? Was she kidding?

I looked at her. "Wanna take my place?" She pulled into the driveway, the tires crunching the pebbles and sand. Immediately, the smell of fire drifted through the car. I peeked at the beach, red, orange, and yellow fire reaching the dark sky and crackling.

We sat there in silence for a few moments until she turned to me and said, "You can do this."

I looked at her with crazy eyes. "What if Hampton isn't here yet?"

"He probably is," she said. "Do you see his car?" I looked around, but it was too dark to tell for sure.

"I don't know," I said. "I can't tell."

"As much as I'd love to sit here for a few hours," she said, and I shot her a look, "I have to get to my brother's recital. You can do this."

"And if I can't?" I asked. It's not like I could've called her. Or my parents, because I needed to prove to them I didn't need Dr. Yao. Maybe I could walk back. It wasn't too far—just a few miles.

"You can," she said.

"Boss-ass-bitch, remember?" I nodded, unconvinced. "You look great." I took a breath, pulled open the door, and stepped out. She gave me a thumbs-up, pulled out of the parking lot, and left.

I turned toward the beach, taking what felt like my one-hundredth deep breath of the night, and started in the direction of the bonfire. The closer I got, the thumping music grew louder and clearer. And so did the faces of every person standing around the fire. The first person who looked my way was Aaron. He had a beer in his hand but seemed less intoxicated since the last time I saw him.

"Party Penny! We meet again," he said, a smile on his face as he started toward me.

"Hey," I said, my stomach soothing a bit. Aaron was a good person to start with. "I've been seeing you out a lot lately." The look on my face made him swallow his swig of beer quickly, shaking his head in reassurance. "I don't mean it in a bad way. I'm happy you're back."

"Thanks."

"You want a drink?" He pointed to the cooler. "We've got beer, seltzers..." Aaron winked at me, wiggling his eyebrows.

"But if I know you, you'd want the harder stuff.

"C'mon," he waved in the direction of his car, "I have some liquor in my car." Liquor. Car.

"Oh, no thanks."

He stopped, looking surprised. "Party-Penny doesn't want vodka? What happened?" My stomach returned to its nervous state, jumping uncomfortably.

"I'm just not in the mood for it tonight," I said, trying my best to smile. The smile I put on for my parents.

"Hey," Justin suddenly cut in, putting a hand on my lower back. "You came." I moved away from his touch, and he frowned. Did he think I came for him? Someone called Aaron's name, and he walked away.

"Yeah," I said. "Do you know where Hampton is?" A look crossed his face, maybe hurt, but he pointed to our left. I looked, and he was chugging a can of beer. In a few seconds, he finished and threw it in the fire. It sputtered in return, the aluminum surely going to remain once the fire diminished. Girls and guys cheered around him, and that's when I spotted Annie. She was grinning, squeezing his bicep. Claire and Jasmine were the closest to Hampton, with Heather and Courtney near the coolers of drinks.

"Do you want some food? There's some burgers and hotdogs," he started, and I turned to him.

"I think I'm gonna go, actually."

"Why?" His face fell a bit. "You just got here." I couldn't

think of a good enough reason other than faking an illness, and even that seemed pathetic to me. I looked back at Hampton, Annie practically hanging on his every word, and I wondered if I was just embarrassing myself. Clearly, they were perfect for each other. Here I was, showing up and thinking I *actually* had a shot.

"C'mon," he said, putting the same hand on my lower back and guiding me toward the food. "I'll make you a burger. Extra cheese and ketchup, right?" He was right. But I wasn't hungry because the closer we came to Annie, the more I wanted to cut and run.

"Penny!" Hampton's voice traveled over the music, and I looked at him. Justin's hand fell off my back, and it was then that the party seemed to still, and everyone's eyes fell on the famous Party Penny. Claire and Jasmine glared from their positions behind Annie, but her eyes darkened at the sight of me. Her smile had disappeared, and her grip on her can of seltzer tightened. But Hampton didn't even notice, or he chose not to notice, as he swiftly moved from her grasp and crossed from his place beside the fire to me.

"You came," he grinned. My stomach, ready to implode, was actually calmed by the look on his face. But just a little.

"Hi," I said. "Yeah, I'm here." I remembered Jess's reminder: *You're a boss-ass-bitch.* I straightened my shoulders, trying to remember, for at least a moment, what it felt like to be the old me. The Fun me. The Confident me.

He grabbed a seltzer from the cooler, cracking it and handing it to me. "For looks," he winked, taking a sip of his own. I smiled, playing with the cap on the drink. Justin had fallen back into the crowd of thirty or so people.

I looked at the can. One sip couldn't hurt. I tipped the drink into my mouth, a familiar bubbling sensation erupting over my tongue and slipping down my throat. I coughed.

Hampton's eyes were wide. "I didn't mean to force anything on you. You don't have to drink that."

"It's okay," I reassured him. "A few sips won't kill me." I slowed, but it killed someone. I was desperate to change the topic. "How long have you been here?"

"Like, twenty minutes."

"So," I started, "is it as fun as you thought it'd be?"

"Maybe after more of these," he held up his beer, giving a smile.

"What's a few?" I asked in a teasing tone, and the ease with which we fell into conversation comforted me.

"Like three," he shrugged.

"Just to get a buzz. I don't really like drinking all that much." I nodded. "Don't get me wrong, I'm all about having fun. But I don't like not being in control."

I wondered if he would really *judge me then. I was once the epitome of not being in control.*

He nudged me. "I've heard you're quite the partier yourself."

"Who'd you hear that from?" My tone dropped, nervous.

Hampton's face grew soft. "Well, if your nickname is Party-Penny…"

Duh. Of course, he would assume I was a partier.

He laughed, squeezing my shoulder. "I'm just kidding." I eyed his hand and wanted him to touch me again. Suddenly, the music quieted a bit.

Courtney stood by the speaker. "Everyone ready to play a game?"

"Game?" Hampton asked me.

I shrugged. "We played 'Truth or Dare' last year. It doesn't last long because people eventually get tired of daring their friends to make out with someone."

"Truth or dare?" he asked, chuckling.

"I haven't played that since seventh grade."

From a few feet away, Miles raised his hand.

Courtney rolled her eyes. "We're not in class, Miles. You don't have to raise your hand."

"I was trying to be polite," he said, gaining a few laughs from his friends.

"What's your question?" She grabbed a drink from the cooler.

"What game are we playing?"

Courtney popped the can and took a sip. "I was getting there. Two truths and a lie. If someone guesses the truth and lies correctly, then you drink." Some nodding erupted over everyone.

"Seems easy enough," Hampton said. Yeah, sure, if it were a game without Annie, the Mets, my ex-boyfriend, and everyone who knew my darkest secret. What couldn't go wrong? But I nodded with a tight smile, following everyone to sit around the bonfire. By the time everyone was seated and ready to go, I eyed the seating arrangement. Annie sat with the Mets on the opposite side of Hampton and I, with Justin on the other side of the circle. Surprisingly, Annie didn't look my way. She whispered to Jasmine, who nodded along to whatever she was saying. I avoided possible eye contact with anyone in the group; I focused my attention on my bare feet in the sand.

Hampton, who sat to my left, leaned closer. His hot breath tickled my ear. "This isn't, like, vicious, right?"

"The game?" I asked.

He nodded. I looked around the circle of my ex-friend group, finally looking back at him. "I hope not." The music lowered just a bit more.

"Okay, Justin, you can go first," Courtney announced.

"Ya know, out of courtesy since you've been watching your ex-girlfriend practically *climb* Hampton."

The Mets giggled; Annie shot me a wink as if saying, "Game on." My face burned, and I was glad for the darkness. I couldn't even look at Hampton. I took a long sip of my drink.

"All right, all right," Justin said, tipping his head to the sky and thinking. He held out three fingers. "I have a dog. I'm going to Wake Forest. And… I'm single." Justin glanced my way for just a second when he said the last one, and I forced myself to not roll my eyes. *Nice one, Justin. Once a masochist, always a masochist.*

"Bo-ring!" Aaron yelled from the other side, smiling.

"Courtney, I thought this game was going to be fun."

"Give it some time," Courtney said back. The Mets laughed at her comment, though I wasn't sure what was so funny about that.

"Well, if you think it's so easy, then answer." Justin laughed.

Aaron sighed dramatically, the beer seeming to get to him. "The lie is that you have a dog, and the truth is you're going to Wake Forest because you've been recruited there since you were eleven." That got a laugh out of the group. Justin was a pretty talented soccer player, and Wake had recruited him when he was a freshman at Royal High. "And the second truth is you being single because we all know Penny dumped your ass." Laughter and sounds of surprise erupted from the group, and Justin held up a middle finger with a frown. He didn't think it was funny. Aaron gave me a friendly, reassuring smile.

"I won. Drink!" Aaron yelled, and Justin drank without complaint. Aaron went next, as dramatic as ever.

"Hm, let's see. I love Grey Goose. I've never had a girlfriend, and I would love to kiss Courtney tonight." We all laughed, and Courtney smiled to herself.

Annie raised her hand. "Easy. The lie is that you've never had a girlfriend; the truth is that you love Grey Goose, and," she paused, smirking, "you'd love to kiss Courtney."

"Kiss Courtney, *when*?" Aaron cupped a hand to his ear, looking for the proper sentence.

Annie rolled her eyes. "You'd love to kiss Courtney *tonight*." The laughter continued.

Aaron jumped up and crossed the circle to Courtney. He pulled her up, drawing her close to his chest and kissing her deeply. Cheers erupted, and by the time they finally pulled apart, Courtney handed her drink to him and said, "Drink." Hampton laughed along with everyone else, and I even found myself laughing. Finally, the commotion settled, and it was Annie's turn.

"Okay," Annie repositioned herself, taking a tiny sip of her drink and thinking.

"I have a little sister; my mom is the Royal High's principal"—a bunch of guys yelled at that one because it was obvious—"and… I wanna sleep with the new kid from New York." I looked at Hampton, who let out a quiet, breathless laugh. He ran a hand through his hair, his face blank. Annie kept a seductive gaze on him, not backing down.

Sarah, a girl from my Spanish class, raised her hand. "Your lie is that you have a little sister, and your truths are that your mom is the principal and that you want to sleep with Hampton."

"I never said his name." Annie shrugged, smirking.

Oh, come on.

"But yes, that's right." She chugged her drink, finishing it and crunching the metal, her eyes still on Hampton's. Sarah told her truths and lies next, and one by one, the whole group had had a turn—besides both Hampton and I.

Hampton was new, so it made sense that he remained. But me? I didn't want to have a turn.

"Wait," Jasmin piped up. "Penny didn't go yet." My stomach dipped and returned to its previously sick state.

"Because she sat there and didn't say anything," Aaron said in a *duh* type of way. I looked at him, wanting to retract my previous warm feelings about him standing up for me.

"Everyone has to go," Jasmine said, looking at me. "That's the fun of it all."

I spotted a bush, thinking it'd be a good place to vomit. "I don't need to. We've been doing this for a while, so I'm sure everyone's tired."

"Sure you do," Annie said, flashing a scary smile at me.

"Party-Penny has to have a go."

"She doesn't *need* to go," Hampton said, voice strong and unwavering.

"C'mon, Penelope." Annie laughed, but I knew it was a fake. "It's just a game. I remember how much you used to *love* games." I swallowed hard, my throat suddenly dry. It was true; when we were fifteen, I still hadn't had my first kiss. Annie had kissed almost half the grade by then, not me. We conspired for weeks on how to get my first kiss, finally settling on planning our very first boy-girl party at my house.

Someone distracted my parents, and a few of us went into the basement to play Spin the Bottle. It was a half-empty plastic ketchup bottle, hardly even worthy of instigating the game, but it was the easiest thing to grab without my parents noticing something was up. I went first, and it landed on Justin. The rest was history.

But this *was* just a game. I could just say stupid things. Plus, Hampton would think something was off if I didn't want to have a turn in an elementary school game.

I pinched the fabric of my sweatshirt.

"Fine. Let me think—"

"I'll help you out," Annie cut in, her voice clear, steady, and strong. I looked at her, alarmed. She wouldn't—

"I used to be popular, but now everyone hates me. I'm desperate enough to think that Hampton will actually be into me because he doesn't know what I did." She said it fast but slowly, right after the other, as if she had rehearsed them. "And I murdered Jack Doe."

Chapter 17

It was quieter than it'd been all night. All voices and movement stopped, and the music continued to play. I stared back at Annie, feeling empty and cold and full of rage all at once.

Aaron let out a whistle. "I thought this was supposed to be a fun game." Justin, looking pissed, shook his head.

"Annie, you're *such* a bitch."

Hampton put a hand on my thigh, but I barely felt it. In a low murmur only I could hear, he said, "Are you okay?"

My head snapped to his, and I searched his face for an ounce of surprise.

Confusion. Anything that suggested he had no idea what Annie was talking about. His tone suggested otherwise. "Why are you acting like you already know?"

Hampton glanced at the sand, took a breath, and then looked back at me without saying a word.

"You're joking," I croaked out, my fingers trembling. Hampton was just shaking his head, putting a hand over mine to try and stop me in my tracks. But it wasn't working. Hampton was just like them: vindictive, manipulative, and immature. *Why did I think he would be any different?*

Right then, I felt my walls come up once again. I stood, crossing through the circle and away from it all.

"Penny!" Hampton yelled after me, but I kept walking. My shoes were back by the coolers, but there was no way I was going back for them.

"Penny, wait," he said, standing beside me and grabbing my hand.

I pulled away, tears streaming down my face. "You knew this whole time? Who told you? Was it Annie? Justin?"

"I didn't tell him anything." Justin suddenly jogged into view.

I knew my mascara was probably streaming down my face. I threw up my hands at the sight of him. "Great! Just what I need right now."

"What does that mean?" Justin asked.

"It means that you're always *there*, and I don't *want* you to be." I was talking fast without a thought of repercussions, but I didn't care.

"Penny." He paused. "Annie is just a bitch who has no idea what she's talking about—"

"You weren't there!" I yelled, cutting him off. The consequences of not visiting Dr. Yao were surfacing. It felt like every part of me was trembling.

Justin looked like he'd been slapped. "So, that's what this is about? You broke up with me because you're mad that I didn't come out and save you from making a mistake."

I forgot Hampton was standing there, watching the explosion between the two of us. It only made me feel more humiliated. I took a breath, shaking my head. "No. But it sure would've helped."

"Unbelievable," he muttered, throwing up his hands in surrender. "Have a nice life, Penny." He backstepped and headed toward the fire.

"Do you want me to drive you home?" Hampton asked, reaching out to me. I pulled back.

"How long have you known? About Jack?"

He shrugged a sad sort of shrug. "Since the first week of school." It was like the wind was knocked out of me. The first week of school? So all that time, he knew that I was a killer.

"So, what?" I laughed shortly without humor. "Did Annie put you up to this? 'Oh, let's play a joke on Penny and have the new guy hang out with her. It'll be hilarious.'"

"What?" He looked confused. "That doesn't even make sense."

"If you knew Annie the way I do, it does."

"I would never do something like that," Hampton said. "And I knew that there's a different side to every story. I'm not stupid." I didn't answer because I couldn't trust anyone. "Do you want to talk about it?"

"No need. You probably already know it better than I do," I said, turning and walking away from him. I wasn't sure how long it would take me to get home, but down the dark beach I went, and headfirst I fell into 11 July.

*

"*See? I told you it wouldn't be too bad,*" Annie said beside me in the passenger seat, taking a swig of her drink. I concentrated on the dead road in front of us; the only thing alive was the flickering of a street light.

"*You're the greatest, Penny,*" Jack said in the backseat, rolling down the window and sticking his head out like a dog.

"*Uh, huh,*" was all I said, turning left onto yet another dead street. McDonald's was up ahead, the only visible light amidst the darkness. Jack started screaming out the window, his arms up.

"*Shh!*" Annie and I both urged, and she rolled up the

window to force him back in.

"Are you stupid? Someone could hear us and call the cops," Annie said, turning to look back at him.

"Stupid but hot," he said behind my seat, giving me a chuckle.

Annie sighed beside me, whispering, "Looks like I'm gonna be ending this sooner than I thought." She and I fell into an easy laugh.

I tripped over a piece of driftwood, falling to the wet sand. It stuck to my palms and knees. I cried harder, knowing what was coming. I pulled myself up from the sand. The flashbacks were vivid. Too vivid. Like I could never escape the night, and it was almost hard to distinguish what was real and what wasn't.

The dark beach before me suddenly became a car, where I sat with Annie and Jack.

"What are you laughing about?" Jack asked.

"Nothing," we chorused, catching each other's eyes and laughing even more.

"Who decided that this"—she tipped her head to Jack—"would be a good idea again?"

"Um, you?" I emphasized pulling into the McDonald's parking lot. The electric yellow and red signs lit up the car.

"Whatever. Let this be a reminder that I shouldn't be responsible for the choices I make about boys," she said, rolling her eyes.

"You should order before he jumps out of the car." I nodded, putting my foot on the gas a little too forcefully. The car lurched forward.

All three of us gasped, and Annie hit my arm. "Are you trying to kill us?"

"I'm sorry," I said, blinking. I guess I was still drunk. I

ordered the food as best as I could; my breath mostly held for the entirety of it, and I rolled the window back up.

Annie giggled as soon as it shut. "You're a legend! Are you even drunk?"

"Yes! I could barely see the screen. We gotta get back." Annie told Jack to pretend he was sleeping so that the McDonald's workers wouldn't suspect a thing. He nodded intensely, shutting his eyes and slumping against the window. There may have even been some fake snoring.

She rolled her eyes at me, and I could already tell she was going to end it tonight. The poor guy had no chance. We paid for the food and were handed a steaming bag of fried goodness. The smell of fries filled the car, and my mouth watered.

Jack took his chicken nuggets from the bag, popping one in his mouth and closing his eyes. "Mmm. Amazing."

"Let's put music on," Annie suggested, connecting her phone to the Bluetooth. In an instant, her music streamed loudly through the speakers.

I tripped again, but this time over my own feet. My hands found the sand again, and my body drained, begging me to stay put. Chest heaving, I blinked at the dark body of water in front of me. The waves, slow, small, and steady, lapped cautiously to maintain the cyclical foundation of the ocean. Determined to the ferocity of its core. Just like my memories. The rushing water reached my bare legs, soaking my jean shorts. I put my face in my hands, tears streaming. My shoulders rose and fell quickly, a familiar sense of panic seizing my chest.

Every fiber of my being pushed against the remainder of the memory. But my mind pursued it. I found myself back in the car.

I turned the music down, dropping the change in the cupholder. "Not yet. I still have to get back. I have to focus."

"Oh, come on," she whined. "You've been cool for exactly ten minutes. Please stay that way."

"What's that supposed to mean?" I turned to her, putting my foot on the break. The car lurched aggressively, and Annie put a hand on the dashboard.

"Jesus, Penny. Drive much?"

I stared, waiting for her to address my question.

She rolled her eyes. "It means that we drove here the entire way in silence, and I want to hear music. Don't you want music, Jack?" She spun the dial, and the music blared.

"I don't feel so good," he said, totally ignoring her question. But I'd been ignoring her aggressive comments all night. I didn't know what made me so confrontational; maybe it was the alcohol, or maybe it was that I'd finally had enough. Regardless, I was over being her punching bag.

"I'm sorry that you forced me to drive while drunk and that I wanted to be somewhat responsible **and keep the music off so I could concentrate.**" I said, sarcasm spilling from my mouth.

She laughed. "Are you joking? I thought you'd have fun. That I could give you this memory that you'd look back on."

"What?" I turned to her. She thought she could give me a memory. How conceited was she? The music blared in the background, and suddenly, Jack was climbing out of the car and vomiting on the pavement. I hadn't even heard his door open.

"I feel better," he said outside the door, kneeling and holding his stomach with one hand and clutching the box of chicken nuggets with the other. Jack smiled a content smile, popping another chicken nugget in his mouth. I cringed at the smell of vomit and fries wafting through my open window. I knew it was never a smell I'd forget.

"Ew," Annie muttered. "I so chose the wrong guy this time."

I looked away from him, turning to Annie. "Why do you have to be such a bitch?"

"What did you just call me?" Her eyes widened. "Fuck you, Penny."

"Excuse me?" We were yelling now, and the music on the speaker seemed to be growing louder and louder in our ears.

"Remember where you came from." She turned toward the window.

"Who do you think you are?" I don't think I'd ever spoken to her like that.

"Everyone barely remembers you were a PB&J, but I remember. And the only reason you're cool is because of me."

"So, what? You want me to get on my knees every day and thank you for getting me to the top of the food chain in high school?" I asked, a new flash of anger I'd never felt toward her pouring over me.

"News flash, Annie. One day, you're gonna wake up and realize that high school is over and the real world has begun. I'd pay money to see how you handle that."

"I want to go back," she said, staring me dead in the eye.

"And you better bet that none of our girls back at the party are gonna take your side." I stared back, my throat burning with rage. I could tell that she was already replacing me, running through potential candidates in her mind. But did I care? Not as much as the idea of me being so disposable.

"Drive!" she yelled, the music reaching its bridge.

"Fine!" I slammed my foot on the gas, earning a loud, horrible thump that ricocheted through the car.

It was then that Jack was suddenly flying; he was suspended over the hood of the car, twisting in the air like a ballerina, and it only took seconds for a betrayal of beautiful form because, *faster than it began, he landed in a heap that lacked the previous elegance. The sound of the impact between his body and crushing metal was deafening; Annie and I's screams were louder than anything I'd ever heard.*

My hands jerked the car into park. My legs jumped out of the seat, racing over the pavement toward him. He laid face down and mangled, specks of deep, red blood splattered over the ground. Chicken nuggets sprinkled the pavement.

"Jack?" I shook his shoulders. "Jack, wake up." He lay motionless on the ground, unresponsive. Tears streamed down my face fast and hard, and I looked for Annie. She sat on the passenger side, staring down at the two of us. Her eyes were wide, fear paralyzing any possible movement she may have had.

"Annie! What are you doing?" I cried, frustrated at her complete lack of urgency. "Call nine-one-one. Now!" At this point, the McDonald's workers had already heard the commotion. They filed out, one by one, running and yelling at one another to do what I had asked of Annie. Amidst all the commotion, she sat still like a statue. Within what seemed like moments, sirens rang through the air and over Annie's music. I sat back, crying. My hands clawed my hair, nails digging into the scalp. Paramedics jogged over to the scene, kneeling and putting fingertips around his neck. His wrist. My eyes lingered over the tangle of limbs, and nausea rose in my stomach and throat. I turned away from the scene, vomiting and covering the blood-speckled ground. Everything that followed was a blur.

Chapter 18

After my breathing returned to normal and the tears slowed, I pulled myself up from the sand and started on my trek home. After what seemed like multiple hours, but in reality was only one, I reached my driveway and practically limped to the door. My feet ached from trudging through the sand and sharp pebbles. By the time the sand met the road, I'd gotten a few strange looks from drivers. Probably deciding whether to stop and help the poor girl with runny makeup and no shoes. I was too much in a daze to care.

It was around twelve. Mom and Dad said they wouldn't go to sleep until I was home, but I crossed my fingers that they were reading in bed.

The lights in the kitchen were off, so a small part of me relaxed. I just wanted to change into comfortable clothes and slip into bed, forgetting the night in its entirety.

And forgetting is what I did best lately. I opened the door to the kitchen, shutting it as softly as I could. Sighing, I leaned back against the door. Finally home.

I walked through the dark and silent kitchen, the smell of Dad's steak still in the air. Turning the corner to where the living room met the stairs, I stopped. Mom sat curled in one of her favorite chairs, illuminated by an overhead lamp, as she read.

She looked up, startled. "Penny! You're home."

I nodded, feeling like I was on the brink of tears again.

"Yeah," I said, heading to bypass her.

"Was it fun?" she asked, closing her book and giving me a tired smile. I wondered why she was downstairs in the first place; Mom went to bed on the earlier side almost every night. Twelve was definitely past the norm.

I tried to not meet her eyes. "Yeah, it was fun."

"Penelope," Mom said, stronger this time, and she rose from her chair.

"Look at me."

I stopped, finally meeting her eyes.

"Honey," she whispered, putting a hand to my face. She eyed my feet, her eyes widening. "Why are your feet so dirty?"

I didn't answer.

"Did you *walk* here?"

I gave a slow nod.

"Where was Jess?" Not responding, I looked at my mom, and something in my chest cracked open. I burst into tears, falling into her and sobbing against her chest. The exhaustion from pretending everything was okay for the past few months was too much to handle. I just wanted someone to hold me, and that's exactly what she did. She put a hand around my back, the other holding my head.

"Shh," she soothed. It felt good to cry. To cry over losing Justin. And Annie. Over Hampton and his betrayal. The embarrassment from the night. And most of all, to cry for Jack.

*

Surprisingly, I slept really well. In fact, I didn't wake up until eleven. I even slept through the smell of Dad's french toast, which were most usually my alarm clock. I laid there for a few moments, staring at the white ceiling. I knew what needed to be done.

I couldn't go on without it any more. By the time I slipped out of bed and changed my T-shirt, I had made my way downstairs to where I knew my parents would be sitting. "Good morning, sleepy head," Dad said as soon as I entered the living room, glancing up from his phone. I'm sure he had to have known what went down last night, but that was Dad. Pretending to act surprised when you told him something he already knew.

"Morning," I said, glancing at Mom. She gave me a smile—a warm, real one—and it was what made me sit on the couch to look at them both. "I want to start seeing Dr. Yao again." My parents looked at each other, having caught them off guard. I was sure they weren't expecting that. But I knew I needed it—to grow past the accident. To drive a car again, guilt-free. To have a sip of alcohol that doesn't remind me of splattered blood and chicken nuggets.

"What brought this on?" Dad asked.

I shrugged, saying the most honest thing I'd said in a while. "I want to feel better," I said, looking at my fingers. "And I know she can help."

Mom nodded. "I'll give her a call today."

"And," I paused, "there's another thing. Can I go see Grandma? Not for long; I just… want a break."

That time, they looked at each other for longer, seeming to have a conversation in moments. Dad took a breath. "Do you think that will help? Getting away?" It almost felt like a rhetorical question, like taking a break from reality wasn't the best decision. I thought about last night, remembering Hampton's face glowing from the reflection of fire. Annie exposing the worst night of my life. And then Hampton **having already known it all.**

I nodded. "Yeah."

"We'll talk it over," Mom said. "What about school?"

"I'm ahead in most of my classes, so I can just talk to my teachers and get the work." The good thing about having little to no friends is that it means excelling as a student. Besides, I needed a break from being me.

My parents exchanged another look, clearly wary about my leaving. "What's the problem?"

Mom looked at me, her gaze concerned. Usually, that type of question would have raised some reprimanding, but something about the way she looked at me that morning was different. She'd seen me break down my shell hours earlier, and maybe she felt almost relieved that I lost it, like it was a reminder that I was, in fact, a human with genuine emotions.

I was still her daughter.

But instead of raising her voice, she pressed her lips together. "I just don't think it's good to think you can just run away from your problems."

"Mom," I cut her off—another thing I would've gotten yelled at for—and shifted on the couch. "Do you know what it's like to be me?" I felt a flash of anger in my chest. I was done with the lies.

She blinked, seeming suddenly unsettled by my question. "I thought you were doing well. I thought your friends—"

"Friends?" I laughed.

"I don't have any friends, Mom. Jess is the only person who stuck by my side, and even she has friends." Both of them scrunched their faces, confused beyond measure. How could you blame them? I'd been feeding them lies for months. But it was time to tell the truth.

Mom gripped her coffee, her knuckles white. "What about that boy? The one who showed up here the other day?" *Hampton.*

"He's nothing," I said.

"So you've been lying to us," Dad finally spoke, his voice cracking. He was always my pal, so I knew that it hurt him to know I'd been lying straight to his face.

I looked down at my fingernails, picking at a hangnail. "I'm sorry."

"What about all the parties you went to?" he asked, clasping his hands over the table. So I told them that instead of being a normal teenager, I'd been going to the cafe down the street with my usual Chai latte and homework. They stared, probably unsure if they should yell or hug me for finally telling the truth.

"I think I should talk to Mrs. Prickett," Mom started.

"We have a good relationship with her; she knows you well, and she'll advise Annie to help you out."

"She hates me." This time, their response was silence.

"Penny," Mom took a pause. "Mrs. Prickett does *not* hate you. She's known you since you were a little girl." *Debatable.*

"I wasn't talking about her," I said.

"I meant Annie."

"What are you talking about?"

"I killed her boyfriend. Did you really think we were going to be having sleepovers and braiding each other's hair?" Mom noticeably flinched from my choice of words, but how else was I supposed to say it?

Mom stood slowly, her gaze set on the floor the entire time. She took a breath, crossed the living room to the front door, and let herself out. She needed a breather and a moment to think, and I knew exactly where she was going. Whenever I was giving her trouble as a kid and she needed a breather, the front steps were always her safe haven.

I stood, following the same path she took. The November air

had a slight bite to it, and I hugged my arms close to my body. I sat on the top step, right next to her, and stared at my chipping nail polish. It was quiet between us for a few minutes. I picked at my nail polish, hearing the sound of wind rustling the trees and filling the empty space around us.

"I'm sorry," I said, breaking the silence. It wasn't just an apology for lying about Annie; it was everything. For lying to her. For fighting with her. For not leaning into her when I needed it most and for shutting her out. Mom put an arm around my shoulders, drawing me into her. I rested my head on her shoulder, inhaling her scent.

Her hair smelled like lilac shampoo, and a flashback of my childhood passed between us. I was little again, and the motion of her carrying me up the stairs lulled me to sleep. My head was always burrowed in her neck, her hair draping over my nose and tickling me. But it had the same smell—lilac.

"I'm sorry, too," she said. My head snapped up, our eyes locking. I was confused. "What are you sorry for?"

For the first time in a while, she seemed to choose her words very carefully. "For not coddling you when it was needed." I blinked, taken aback. She took my hands in hers.

"That's what I'm sorry for." My eyes burned, tears threatening to spool over my eyelids.

"I'm going to call Dr. Yao today and set up an appointment," she squeezed my hands. "I'm proud of you." A tear finally succeeded and slipped over my cheek, others following in an orderly fashion.

"And I'm sorry that you lost Annie, too. I know how close you were." She gave my hand one last squeeze, rising and stepping back into the house.

I returned my attention to my chipped nails, my lips pressing firmly into a frown. Mom never saw the bad things about Annie, or at least I didn't tell her. Even though it was a small town, she didn't know that she was one of the meanest girls in school or someone who would use boys for a few weeks and then throw them away. She didn't know she made me feel less than most of the time. I paused. Maybe because sometimes, while also feeling dejected by Annie's behavior, I also felt on top. High from the attention the coolest girl in school gave me.

A piece of polish was scraped off, floating to the ground. I made a vow to stop lying, but why did it feel like I still was? And who exactly was I lying to?

Chapter 19

Dr. Yao's office was calming. The artsy floral arrangements resting on her desk hadn't changed since the last time we'd met; on one side of her tidy table, an ivy drooped over the sides of a gray pot. Next to it sat the familiar-looking succulents I'd already seen. The only difference is that they were a tad larger, and I managed a half-smile. Maybe I understood the appeal of being a plant mom.

My attention was mostly on the other side of the table; in a black square pot, tiny white pebbles laid the groundwork for a criss-cross-looking plant. It was new. Strikingly knew.

"It's a bamboo plant," Dr. Yao said, addressing my wandering eyes. "My husband got it for me as a gift."

"I like it," I said, taking my eyes away from the wild-looking plant. She took a breath, closing the black notebook on her lap and tucking it to the side of her chair. I guess she wasn't going to be taking notes. I relaxed a tiny bit, my shoulders lowering from their hitched position.

"So the bonfire," she started slowly. "Want to tell me about it?" Mom must've mentioned it over the phone; I'd only been there for ten minutes, and we'd sat quietly without much deep discussion.

I shrugged. "Jess brought me, and I guess I was excited for it."

"Any particular reason?" Immediately, I thought of him.

I shrugged. "Not really." Her gaze lingered behind her

tortoise-shell-rimmed glasses.

"What happened when you got there?"

"I saw Justin. I didn't want to see him, though. He's just always," I tried to find the words, "a lot. All the time. And he doesn't understand that I don't want to be with him."

"Well, why don't you want to be with him?"

"Because." I paused, thinking of what I'd said to him. And how hurt he looked. It was because of what I did and how, since I already pulled Jess down with me to suffer the life of ostracization, I couldn't be selfish enough to pull him down as well. So I told her, and she listened patiently.

"Did you ask him what he wanted?" Dr. Yao asked.

"No, but only because I already know what he wants—to be with me."

"Have you ever let him express himself completely to you?"

I thought, shaking my head. *No, I hadn't.*

"You have to think of the perspectives. Yes, you feel that way. But he may feel differently. Do you feel guilty that Jess is still your friend?" I nodded a small nod, the familiar swirl of discomfort forming in my belly.

"But that's her choice," she said. "She chose to remain friends with you, and even though others didn't, it doesn't mean you need to feel guilty about it." She smiled a soft smile.

"I'll tell you a secret that my mom always told me. The ones who stick around, even through hardships, are your real friends. As for Justin," she continued, taking a breath.

"Trauma affects everyone differently. For some in a relationship, the trauma might actually bring them closer. For others, it may bring them apart. For you, Penny, do you think the car accident changed your feelings toward Justin? Or do you feel that because of this incident, you're not good enough to be loved?

It's not fair to have a boyfriend and be happy when Jack can't." I stared, uncomfortable and feeling like she'd read my mind.

Dr. Yao pressed her lips together, giving me a tiny shrug. "I think once you figure out why you feel the way you do, giving Justin an explanation might help the situation." I guess I'd never given him a chance to understand where I was coming from. I did love Justin; I knew that. But I didn't love him the way I did before.

"He might not even let me explain," I said, frowning. "I told him the reason we couldn't be together was because he didn't come out of the house and save me that night."

"Save you from what?"

I looked her in the eyes, feeling sick, and saying it. It was my fault alone, and I never should have put the blame on him. "From driving. I guess I just always knew he would be there for me, no matter what, and when he wasn't…" I trailed off, hoping she'd get the gist of what I was saying.

"When he wasn't, your subconscious couldn't handle it all being your fault, so it chose someone close to you that could share some of the burden." She uncrossed her legs, leaning forward.

"I think we've already made progress."

"How?"

"Because you unintentionally told me about one of your coping mechanisms. That's huge."

*

By the time I left Dr. Yao's office and was driven home by Dad, my room felt a little different. I still cuddled into bed like I usually did, peering out the window and watching the sun dip toward the trees. But that time, I didn't wish for it to go faster; I was hopeful for the following day because that was when Dr. Yao would uncover more. I found myself crossing my fingers, feeling just a tad lighter, if that were even possible.

After having dinner with Mom and Dad and discussing trivial things like how the weather was supposed to be for the week, we skipped over my therapy session and what'd been discussed. I slipped into bed after dinner, feeling emotionally drained from the day. I stared at the dark ceiling of my room and the sound of the wind whistling outside the window. I pulled the covers toward my chin; it would be getting colder soon. With what felt like hours, my eyes finally slid shut. But one thing remained, and the all-too-familiar reappearance of Jack, twisting in the air and landing on the ground, played on my eyelids. My screams. Annie's frozen face. The sirens.

And I was jolted awake.

*

I told myself that I had to walk into school, regardless of what had happened on the beach. So what if Hampton turned out to be a bad guy? We were leaving in a few months, venturing out into the world, so it only worked in my favor now that he was out of my life. Good riddance, am I right? I parked Shirley on the bike rack, her purple and white swirls contrasting against the black bike beside it.

I pushed open the doors of Royal High. The sounds of rustling students and their voices immediately magnified in my ears. I found my locker in no time, twisting my combination in. Plus, the day wasn't about Hampton. It was about Justin.

Someone with cold fingers suddenly grabbed my arm,

twisting me toward them.

Jess stood, looking good with her hair thrown into a messy bun. Pieces escaped the bun, giving her an effortless but chic look. But I knew she wasn't intentionally going for that. I knew she had just thrown her hair up without a second thought and looked amazing anyway.

"Are you going to tell me what happened at the bonfire or pretend nothing happened?"

I sighed, slipping books into my open bag. "I'm sorry I didn't call you."

"Did you *walk* back?" she asked, raising a questionable eyebrow.

"I heard rumors." I avoided her gaze, knowing she'd be mad at me for not calling her in the state of emergency.

"Like that's new." I rolled my eyes.

"Rumors in Port Royal."

"I didn't believe them. Not until I hear it from you," Jess said, folding her arms. "Tell me what happened." So I did. And she nodded slowly the whole time, scoffing when I told her what Annie said.

"Why does she have to be so…?" She searched for the right word to describe Annie, but I finished it for her.

"Because it's Annie." We nodded together, turning and walking down the hallway together.

"So what happened with Hampton?"

"What do you mean?" I asked, staring ahead.

"Well, what happened after that whole thing? Did he text you?"

I shrugged, my packed backpack weighing my shoulders down. "Why should he? He accomplished what he wanted to."

A girl jogged past me, her arm brushing mine. "Wait, I don't get it. What was he trying to accomplish?" She asked, trying to lock eyes with me. I stared straight ahead, not wanting to rehash any of it. We reached our classroom, finding our seats and slipping into them.

I pulled out a textbook. Jess just looked at me, waiting for an answer. I opened my notebook, turning to a clean page. "Isn't it obvious?"

"Either I'm really slow today or you're speaking in riddles," she deadpanned, frowning.

I wrung my hands together, heaving a big sigh. "I was clearly set up. He knew about the accident before he even met me, and he pretended not to know about it when we hung out. I'm sure Annie and the Mets put him up to it, seeing if they could get the new guy to trick me and laugh behind my back."

Jess just stared, her dark and perfectly waxed eyebrows drawn together in confusion. "Wait. Back up," she paused while the teacher entered the room and passed our desks. "Did he say that he set you up?"

"No," I said.

"Did he say that Annie told him to be friends with you just so that they could laugh about it?"

"No."

She pushed down the top of her pen, earning a *click!* "Did he say anything that suggested he was lying?"

"Well, no," I said, frustrated by her lack of understanding. *Wasn't it obvious?* She just didn't get it.

"Then I'm confused," Jess said, frowning. "He probably didn't mention Jack, so you could tell him yourself. It sounds like he was being thoughtful of your feelings."

"You just don't get it." I shook my head. "It's not like that. Trust me." I turned my attention to the front of the classroom, willing for the teacher to begin speaking and break Jess's gaze that burned into my temple. And he did; for the rest of the class, I avoided talking or even glancing in her general direction. *I knew what Hampton was doing, and I wasn't in the mood to explain something so painfully obvious.*

Chapter 20

I spotted Justin from my position at our lunch table; he was sitting at his own table in the Westside, Hampton, nowhere to be seen. Justin's usual friends sat around him.

Jess waved a hand in front of my eyes.

"What are you looking at?" she asked, taking a bite of her sandwich and munching slowly.

"I need to talk to Justin," I said, my heart thudding against my chest. I'd hope he'd listen.

Jess stopped chewing and swallowing hard. "Do you mean Hampton?"

"What? No," I shook my head, rising from our table. "Be right back." I sped off without a second glance, trying to ignore the swirling feelings in my tummy. Dr. Yao told me to be direct with Justin and be generous enough to give him room to talk. She also gave me some tips on controlling the anxiety I'd get when approaching danger zones like the Westside, but I was still working on that. *Breathe in, breathe out. In, out*—I stopped at his table, ignoring the eyes of the guys who used to be *our* friends.

"Hey," I said.

"Hi," he said. That was Justin; as much as I hurt him at the bonfire, he would put it aside and acknowledge that what I was doing was a big step for me. The Mets were sitting at the table beside them, and they even looked up to witness the latest piece of drama for the day. Annie's hazel eyes skimmed the situation, and I half-expected her to stand and tell me to get lost, but she sat with no malice and simply watched. If my heart wasn't beating a million miles a second, I would've stopped and appreciated the peaceful moment.

"Can we talk?" I stared into his calm eyes. The same eyes I fell for freshman year when he asked me to Creamy & Creamier Creamery and paid for my vanilla bean and blackberry swirl. Every time.

He held my gaze for a moment, contemplating whether to even give me the time of day, but nodded and rose from his seat. His friends made not-so-quiet remarks, but I turned and led the way regardless. I wasn't expecting to be treated nicely. We walked out of the coordinate plane, down a hallway, and out the exit door. We ended up behind the school. Looking around, I could've slapped myself. We were at our makeout spot.

He snickered to himself.

"I'm sorry, I didn't even think about it." He stopped me with a slight shake of his head. I crossed my arms over my chest, then freed them and leaned against the wall. I mentally prepared my next words, silence stretching between us.

"What do you want to talk about? I have class in ten minutes," he said.

"I just…" I paused, ditching perfection and deciding to just speak. "I'm sorry for never giving you the chance to talk to me." He blinked.

"For never letting you console me after Jack. And for never checking in on you…" I trailed off, and he dipped his head.

"I know he was your friend, too." I took a deep breath. "I broke up with you initially because I told myself it wasn't fair for me to bring you down with me, but I think the real reason is that I hated myself too much to even think about loving you."

"Why didn't you let me help you?" he asked.

"All I could think about was what I'd done," I said. "When people started hating me too, it was just too much to handle." Justin pressed his lips together. "I should've talked to you the way I'm talking to you now, and I know I'm way late, but," I shrugged, giving a watery smile, "I'm here now."

He put his fingers to the bridge of his nose, squeezing and letting go. "I can't imagine what that night was like for you. And I'm sorry for not coming outside."

"No," I said forcefully. "What I said to you at the bonfire was wrong. Don't ever be sorry for not stopping me because I chose to drive all on my own. That was all me."

He looked suddenly angry, muttering, "I'm sure Annie had a lot to do with it."

I shook my head. "It was still my choice." He didn't respond, his jaw clenched.

I paused for what I was about to say, not wanting him to take it the wrong way, but it had to be said. "I *really* was in love with you. I don't want you to ever doubt that." Justin lifted his sweet gaze to mine, taking a step forward to close the gap between us.

"I still love you," he said, and it gave me chills. I never pictured myself standing in front of him and hearing those words again; sure, he'd told me over the phone. But that was different. Surprisingly, it felt good in a nostalgic way. My heart ached for the feeling of having been in love with him because that sort of thing never really leaves you. It takes a piece of your heart, a tiny sliver, to rope it off for potential new lovers to respect the boundaries and stake their own territory. They had their own place, but your first love is something special. That was Justin for me, but my heart was big with lots of open spaces.

He reached out to me, taking me in a soft hug. My arms snaked around his back, clutching him. The hug felt like it was long overdue, but while something about it felt good, the same part felt foreign. Justin pulled back slightly, his mouth grazing the top of my ear. His hands found my sides, pulling me closer. He tipped my mouth to his lips until I put a hand on his forearm and pulled back. His grip on my waist loosened.

"I can't kiss you," I said, shaking my head. His head tilted, searching for an answer. "Too much has happened between us."

"We can make it better. I know we can," Justin said, his voice offering an ounce of hope that I didn't have myself.

"Justin," I started. "I don't feel that way toward you any more." He dropped his hands, sighing through his nose.

"I need to figure out so many things, and it can't start like this." It took a moment, but his features softened.

"Have you talked to Annie about what happened with Jack?"

"No," I said, blinking. "Why?"

"I think it would help," was all he said, but there was no way I was going to approach Annie and suggest a kumbaya. He hugged me again, but it felt different this time. Less soft. Quicker. He put a hand on the back of my head, kissing my forehead. "I'm glad we talked. Friends?"

"Of course," I said, and when he entered back through the door, a little piece of the weight on my shoulders chipped. And I felt better.

Chapter 21

A knock sounded on my door.

"Come in," I said, tearing my eyes away from my history notes. Dad stood in the doorway, smiling his excited smile. It was a Sunday—French toast day. I sniffed the air, not smelling the familiar cinnamon and nutmeg. I wonder what he was so excited about.

"What?" I asked, a smile of my own stretching my lips. Seeing Dad excited was like watching a golden retriever retrieve its first tennis ball.

"Mom and I have a surprise for you," he said.

"What is it?"

"It's in the kitchen," he said. "So you have to come downstairs." I slid off my bed, following Dad. He practically hopped down our staircase, letting me enter through the doorway first.

"Surprise!" Mom threw up her hands, waving them like spirit fingers.

I blinked at Grandma, who, with gifts in hand, threw me a huge grin. I took her in, and even though I hadn't seen her since last Christmas, she still looked the same. Maybe with a few more wrinkles under her eyes, but the same wild Grandma. Her leopard sweater accented her dyed-blonde hair, pulled back into a low bun, a matching leopard ribbon flowing from it. She loved her ribbons and, for years, gifted me the same ones so I could match with her. If only you could see our childhood photos together.

Apparently, Grandma looked exactly like me when she was younger. From the moment I started to look like her, she'd give me an outfit that was identical to hers, and Mom made me wear them every time we'd be at family events. Holidays, birthdays—you name it. For years, we looked like weird twin sisters with a huge age gap. Jess laughed at the pictures all the time, begging to see them. But not me; it still gave me the shivers. Now, that was real PTSD.

"Penelope, sweetheart," she said, giving me a hug. She still smelled like a distinct Burberry perfume, but I wasn't sure which one. "Oh, I'm so excited to see you." She pulled back.

"When your parents called and said you wanted to see me, I just had to jump on a flight and come right over." *My parents… called her?*

I looked at them, but they looked so happy that I wanted to mirror their happiness. Or at least pretend to. Okay, let's get one thing straight: I loved my grandma. I *was* happy she was there, but I wanted to visit her in order to get away from Port Royal. I wanted to get on a plane and fly far, far away to Arizona. Didn't anyone understand that?

The three of them jumped straight into a lively chatter, and Grandma placed the gifts on the kitchen table beside her. "So, Penelope, what should we do today?" Mom and Dad both smiled at me, awaiting my answer. So, they hired Grandma as a babysitter.

"How about we do something all together?" I suggested. "We can go to the beach. Or the pier."

"I have to go to the grocery store," Mom said.

"Get some things to make dinner for Grandma." I looked to Dad, practically crying for help.

"I have to do some work for a client today," he said, reaching for Grandma.

"See you later, Mom. You girls have a good day." They left us alone in the kitchen.

"Looks like it's just us." I gave her a nod, wondering what this was all about.

"Maybe go get dressed, and I'll whip up some eggs. Fried, okay?" Another nod, and out of the room I went.

"Try not to look so excited!" she added, but a laugh lay in her tone.

*

"Would you like to drive?" she asked, dangling the keys to her rental car. I avoided her gaze. I grabbed two plastic water bottles from the fridge, dropped them in a plastic bag, and let her take the driver's seat.

"I don't even think that's allowed," I said. "Isn't there an age requirement?" Grandma caught her reflection in the hall mirror, turning sideways and fluffing up her leopard ribbon.

"No one listens to those anyway," she said, still trained on the ribbon.

"Better safe than sorry." I avoided her gaze. I didn't want to get on the topic.

Dr. Yao and I hadn't yet discussed my wishy-washy feelings toward driving, and I'd rather let a professional analyze my brain. Grandma drove, not pushing the topic any further. She knew full well that I'd been using Shirley as my main source of transportation. I didn't have a car prior to the accident, so it's not like I had a constant reminder sitting in my driveway. The car was coupled with my silence and Grandma's chatter, but I had to admit that in ten minutes, she had me grinning over her and the neighbor she was crushing over.

"We get along quite well, and I invite him in sometimes to chat over some cookies and tea," she said, hitting the steering wheel.

"But he doesn't talk much, so that makes me think that he's just being polite with my invitation." Grandma had one of the biggest personalities I knew, and sometimes it was hard for us to sneak in some words with her. I assumed it was the same with her neighbor.

"How many times has he come over?" I asked.

"Seven," she said almost immediately.

"No, wait. That's wrong. I had to cancel one day because the cookies didn't come out right. Six. He's been over six times." I hid my smile over the cookie comment; apart from her boisterous personality, Grandma was quite the perfectionist. If something wasn't just right, the whole operation was scratched.

"I think he likes you," I said, gripping my seat belt.

"I just can't tell!" A pause filled the car, an unusual break from the constant chatter.

"Do you ever have trouble with that?"

"Well—"

"Oh, that's right," Grandma says, shaking her head as if she couldn't believe she'd ask such a silly question. "Your generation is pretty transparent. No guessing."

"I don't know, Grandma. I think it just depends," I said, looking out the window.

The docks whizzed by, boats bouncing in the water. "Do you have any boyfriends?"

"Boyfriends?" I asked, smiling. "As in plural?"

"Yes, that's exactly what I mean." She nodded. "I always had multiples when I was your age. It's more fun that way. Up until I met your grandad, of course." This time, Grandma fell into a beat of thoughtful silence. "He was special." Grandad had passed away when I was in elementary school. I remembered a lot of tall relatives standing above me, crying and hugging each other. A lot of it was really a blur, except for the bright, hot pink ribbon in Grandma's hair at the funeral. I remember it clearly because of the way it stood out from the mass of black, adding a bit of happiness to the somber atmosphere.

"No, I don't know if I have any boyfriends," I finally said after an appropriate amount of silence had passed. "Not even one." I thought of Hampton, suddenly feeling like I was telling a white lie. The idea shocked me because Hampton was far from a boyfriend. He was far from even being a friend. I bit my lip, wondering why he jumped to my mind before Justin would have.

"I don't believe you," she said in a sing-song voice. "Your face told me otherwise." I shook my head, not in the mood to relive some bornfire trauma. The car suddenly pulled into a lot, making the familiar sound of gravel crunching against the tires. I looked around, realizing we were at Moe's. A good number of people milled about. The usual anxiety that settled into my tummy was slight. Maybe it was because I was with Grandma. Or the three therapy sessions I'd already been through. Either worked.

"Why are we here?" I asked.

"I figured I could get something for dinner." She held her purse snugly to her chest.

"Mom's getting food," I said, suspicious.

"Well, you have to admit, dear," she patted my arm. "Your mom's food isn't the best." I let out a laugh, the first time I'd heard of such. I mean, her food wasn't *great*. But it wasn't bad.

I shut the door, finding my place next to Grandma as we

started toward the market. "So, let's see. I'm thinking of spaghetti squash. Do you like spaghetti squash?" I wish I could've given spaghetti squash more thought, but he caught my eye.

Hampton was ambling over the grass with something in his hand.

"Penny," she snapped her fingers in front of my eyes. "Spaghetti squash?"

"Uh, I'm not sure if I've had it. But that sounds great." I nodded, my attention still fixed on the uber-attractive, dirty blonde boy.

Grandma, old in age but quick in senses, followed my gaze. "Oh, he's *cute*. Do you know him?" *No.* The last thing I needed was for Grandma to jump into Hampton and I's... situation. If I could even call it that, abort immediately.

"Let's go get the spaghetti squash," I said, taking her arm and steering her away.

"Penny, there's no need to be nervous around boys." She eyed him again.

"Even if they look like that."

"Spaghetti squash sounds really good right now," I said, attempting to pull her away again.

"Even if I'm not exactly sure what it is," Was it a type of pasta? Or vegetable. I wanted to talk to whoever created the name.

"Penny?" His voice pulled me back into reality, and I turned.

"Hi," I said. We hadn't talked since the bonfire. I hadn't even really seen him at school.

"Hey," he said, shifting from one foot to the other, looking at Grandma, and holding out a hand.

"Hi, I'm Hampton."

Grandma could not look happier, and I could tell she was leaving the majority of it inside. She held out her hand, shaking it. "Judy Brooks, it's a pleasure to meet you." Hampton smiled, returning the gesture.

"Are you one of Penny's boyfriends?" she asked, shooting me a glance like the top-notch wing woman she was. Dear God, please bless me with teleportation skills.

But he laughed, shaking his head. "No, ma'am, I'm not the boyfriend. He's blonder than I am." They laughed together like it was a joke.

"Well, I'm going to go look for some spaghetti squash. I'll just be over there, Penny." And she was off before I could object, leaving me alone with Hampton.

He shifted again, meeting my eyes and managing a half-smile. "How are you?" *Right. The last time he'd seen me was with a mascara-drenched face, having a total meltdown and stomping down the dark beach.*

"I'm good," I said, relaxing. "How are you?" His shoulders seemed to droop a little from the shitty conversation, so he nodded slowly.

"I'm good." It was then that I noticed what he was holding: a bag of chocolate-covered potato chips from Ben's stand, this time tied with a nicer ribbon than the usual twine.

"Listen, I've been meaning to talk to you. I wanted to give you some space, so that's why I waited a little." I blinked, sensing he had more to say.

"I'm really sorry for last weekend. We were having so much fun, and then that stupid game started. I never expected anything like that to happen. What Annie did…" he finished it with a shake of his head, his jaw tense.

"Thanks for saying all that."

"Wait, I'm not done." I stopped, letting him continue.

"I knew about the car accident on my first day at Royal High. Principal Prickett told my mom and me."

My lips parted in shock, confused. "Why would she do that?"

"I don't know," he shrugged. "It was after you'd walked away."

"So she meant it as a warning? To not get within ten feet of me," it came off sarcastically, but I knew, from the bottom of my heart, that that was what she meant.

"Then why would she suggest I show you around for your first day?"

Hampton looked unsure. "It's pretty obvious that she and her daughter come from the same cloth," he said.

"Actually, not a cloth. A rag. A dirty rag with holes in it." I actually smiled because, for a moment, I forgot what we were talking about.

"I didn't tell you about it when we were hanging out because I assumed it was something you didn't want to talk about, and I also figured you would tell me yourself when you felt comfortable."

So, Jess was right. Shit.

"That was nice of you." I crossed my arms.

"Thank you." I tilted my head, curious. "I thought you were hooking up with her at one point."

"Principal Prickett?" he asked jokingly.

"She's not my type." I rolled my eyes, smiling.

"No, Annie."

"She tried pretty hard," he admitted. "But I told her it wasn't gonna work out. I liked someone else."

I nodded, changing the subject. "I'm sorry I yelled at you on the beach. Not my finest moment. I should've heard you out, and it wasn't fair of me to attack you like that."

"It's okay," he said, then pressed his lips together. "Aren't you gonna ask who I was into?"

"I figured it was your business." Grandma was appearing in view—a bag with something that seemed to weigh it down.

He nodded a slow nod, one weighed with a million different thoughts I wished I could know. "I'm glad you're with Justin, by the way. He really cares about you." My body froze. Did I just hear him, right? Me and… Justin? Where did he get that from?

She reached us before I could say anything else, grinning. "I found spaghetti squash."

"Yum," I said, looking at Hampton and wishing I could ask him to clarify, but what only came out was, "we're having spaghetti squash."

"I figured." He laughed, looking at my wingwoman.

"It was so nice to meet you, Mrs. Brooks."

"Miss," she corrects him, taking his hand. "I'm on the market now."

Oh, my god.

"But it was nice to meet you too, Hampton."

"I'll see you around," he said, eyes locked on mine as he stepped through us to the parking lot. My stomach shrunk as his back retreated from us, and I wanted to run after him and question him to death, but I didn't even think Grandma would be a supporter of that one.

*

That night, Grandma exercised her skills in convincing and managed to add the spaghetti squash to Mom's menu. I could tell

Mom wasn't thrilled, but Grandma was too happy to turn her down. After sitting down through a meal of bolognese pasta, Caesar salad, and drum roll, the outlier of spaghetti squash, we settled into the living room to watch a movie. I'd been pretty antsy and annoyed since I found out Justin was my apparent boyfriend. I'd wanted to text him lengthy paragraphs, but I decided I should just chew him out when I saw him at school tomorrow.

I think I would be left more satisfied. Plus, by the time we'd gotten back from the farmer's market, I dialed Jess and debriefed Hampton and I's entire conversation. While she said she hadn't heard once that Justin and I were back together, she agreed that I should wait until tomorrow to find Justin and demand why this was an idea in anyone's head. My guess was that he was telling people, and if that were the case, it was not going to end well for him.

"Earth to Penny?" Dad said, and by the looks of his face, it seemed like he'd been repeating it for a while.

"Sorry," I said. "What?"

"We were just saying we wanted popcorn, and you make it the best." He gave me his best smile. I rolled my eyes because it didn't take a rocket scientist to pop a bag in the microwave for the intended time, but I got up from the couch anyway. The ants in my legs needed to walk around and let off some energy.

I crossed the living room into the kitchen, grabbed a bag, and popped it into the microwave. The bag turned around and around, slowly expanding as the kernels popped and filled the space. Suddenly, a pair of headlights flashed from the corner of my eye. I poked my head around the corner, walked to the front door, and pulled it open. I watched a car retreat down my driveway, pulling away from the street. I stepped forward, confused, until my toe crunched something loud. I looked down, and a bag of Ben's chocolate-covered potato chips was sitting on the ground. The same bag that Hampton had in his hands at the market. It had the familiar, pretty ribbon that I'd admired.

I frowned, looking around for anything else that might offer some more explanation, but found nothing and let myself back inside. Back in the kitchen, the microwave was still going. I peered at the bag in my hands, the kernels in the microwave popping loudly. *Had Hampton dropped this off? And what's with the dramatics? Why didn't he just give it to me at the market?*

I turned it in my hands, my eyes catching a tiny message scrawled in black, inky pen. I peered closer at the boyish handwriting, and it read: *It was you.*

Chapter 22

I thrust Shirley into the bike rack, tightening my hands over my backpack straps and marching to the door. My feet pounded against the ground, and I don't remember the last time I entered the school with that amount of urgency. Actually, I didn't think others did either. I could feel heads turning, watching curiously as the town's murderer—the town's *angry* murderer—marched for her next kill.

And it was true; I was on the hunt for Justin.

I'd gone over and over in my head last night about Hampton's gift, finally figuring out that it was me; *I* was the girl he was into, no one else. But before I could get happy about it, I turned angry. Justin was the reason for Hampton's receding headlights, refusing to stick around and gifting the chips to me himself.

I passed my locker, making my way to his. Down the long row of gaudy yellow metal, my eyes zeroed in. Adrenaline coursed through my veins, my heart thumping rhythmically with every step I took. *Who did he think he was, telling people we were dating?* Boy, wait till Dr. Yao hears this one. No more excuses or sympathy for him.

"Penny?" Someone said my name, but the pumping blood was too thick and fast in my ears. I kept walking, but it was repeated.

"Penny? What's wrong?" Jess suddenly caught up to me, jogging a little to catch up and stay at my pace.

"I can't talk," I said. She grabbed me, yanking my arm to a stop.

"Hey!"

"Where are you going?" She peered closer. "You have this crazy look in your eye."

"I need to shut down this rumor. Now."

"Well." She moved her iced coffee from one hand to the other, "Maybe try to do it without looking like a crazy person."

Jess looked around, leaning closer and whispering, "People are staring."

"Staring? At me?" I put a hand to my heart. "I'll never survive."

Jess rolled her eyes, slapping my arm. "Shut up. Plus, I heard the soccer team has been going in for early practices. He's probably in the athletic center."

I stared, unwavering.

"Which is far away. At the other end of the school."

"Okay." I nodded, turning on my heel and heading in that direction.

I guess I'd be late for English that morning—I was stopped again.

"You are *not* going into the locker room," Jess said.

"I won't let you do that." The warning bell rang, signaling we had a few minutes to get to class.

I scowled at the ceiling, irritated. "I'm losing time."

"You are not going into the boy's locker room to find Justin," she said, and just when she did, a junior passed us and said, "Ow, Ow, Penny Brooks, keep it in your pants!" before laughing and dabbing up on his friends, convinced they were world-class comedians.

Jess held up her finger, turning to me and throwing an arm

around my shoulder. "We're gonna go to English, and then I'll see you at lunch. You can talk to him then." I sighed, the tangle of anticipation settling in my tummy.

"Fine," I said. "But I'm not going to concentrate on anything until then." She laughed, and we walked to class.

"So I have to ask," she started, eyeing me. "Since when do you care what people think about you? Especially if it's someone thinking you have a boyfriend." *Hampton.* Because Hampton told me that I was the girl he turned down Annie for, he delivered chocolate-covered potato chips to me on my front steps like a perfect, chivalrous romance movie, but then burst the bubble by congratulating me on a boyfriend I didn't know I had.

I looked at her, contemplating spilling the beans but knowing I had to. She was my best friend, and she called it from the first day. "If I tell you, you can't tell me that you told me so. Or freak out and cause a scene."

"I'm pretty sure your warfare path this morning has already caused a scene." Jess took a sip of her coffee, swallowing loudly.

"Spill." I looked around us, stopping right before entering our classroom, and pulled her close to me. In her ear, I whispered his name. That was enough detail for the time being.

Jess jumped back from me like she'd been bit, her coffee dropping to the floor and exploding over the gross, speckled linoleum floor. She held her hands to her open mouth, eyes wide, and not a care in the world that she'd dropped her beverage of survival.

"I want to scream," she said, bouncing. "Tell me everything. Right now."

"I said you couldn't cause a scene," I angry-whispered.

"This is scene-worthy!" Jess said back, with, I swear, five exclamation points.

"Miss Brooks? Miss Hunter? Is there a problem?" Our teacher called from inside, peering over the desk.

"Uh," I said. "Jess dropped her coffee by accident, so we were going to clean it up." We were waved off to go do so, so we dropped our bags at the door and headed to the bathroom for cleanup supplies.

"Tell me everything." She grabbed my arm, practically yanking it out of its socket. We fell into the bathroom door, grabbing paper towels from the dispenser. I peeked under the stalls, and the coast was clear.

"He basically told me that Annie tried really hard to hook up with him, but he liked someone else instead," I said, swiping a piece. The whirring sound of the paper as it reloaded filled the room.

Jess poked me in the side. "Wonder who he liked."

"Well, I didn't know," I explained, grabbing another piece and adding it to the growing pile in my hand. "Until he dropped off chocolate-covered potato chips from Ben's at my front door last night, with a little message saying," I motioned for emphasis, "it was you."

She dropped a hand on her forehead, closing her eyes. "He's a romantic, too."

"But then he said that he's happy I'm with Justin."

"Seriously?"

Her eyes were wide, totally engrossed in the soap opera I called my life. I wet a paper towel, squeezing the excess water out and imagining my hands on Justin's throat—kidding. "Seriously."

She nodded, leaning against the sink. "So you think he *told* Hampton you two were dating?" I shrugged, unsure. I just figured I'd go to the source. "Well, I guess you'll find out today," the door swung open, revealing Mrs. Prickett in the flesh. Just from seeing her, I remembered everything Hampton told me the day before. A ball of hatred formed in my belly.

"What are you two doing?" she asked, her tone suggesting an involvement in paraphernalia. Mrs. Prickett, the detective, ladies and gentlemen.

"I spilled my coffee, so Penny and I are getting stuff to clean it up," Jess informed her, knowing our rocky relationship.

"I don't see why Penny needs to help you with that," she said, raising an eyebrow and zeroing in on me. I stared back, refusing to let her gaze bring me down.

"I'll go to class," I said with grace, choosing the high road. I handed the mound of paper towel sheets to Jess.

"Just because you two are seniors does not mean you can slack off from class," Principal Prickett said as I passed her into the hallway. I rolled my eyes because being a senior meant *exactly* that.

*

I scanned the lunchroom like a hawk circling its prey. Jess sat beside me and had abandoned her sandwich, feeling my energy. She had a front-row seat to what was about to go down, and I felt good about being less of a zombie and more like friends who schemed together.

"There he is," she murmured, tapping my arm and pointing to the front door. He swaggered in, bro-hugging some guy. Hampton was already seated at his table, and *God*, he looked good. I felt myself getting lost in his face. He liked me at one point, and I was assuming he still did, considering the potato chips, but nothing could progress further—not until I ended my supposed relationship. My head whipped back to Justin, zeroing in. I watched him cross the coordinate plane and head to the Westside. He would usually get to his table first, chat a bit with his friends, then get food once the line lessened. Smart boy, but I knew his moves before he even made them. I would've stifled a yawn because he couldn't be more predictable than when we were together, but I was on too high of an alert.

"He's on the move," Jess said, and I wasted no time. I rose to my feet, crossing the plane and reaching him.

I grabbed his arm. "Can I talk to you?"

Justin looked at me. "Two times in a week, I'm one lucky guy." His smile faded once it wasn't reciprocated. I turned away, walking out of the lunchroom and into the hallway. No one would be in the hallway at that time since students were either in a class period or eating lunch. The door shut behind us, and he leaned against the wall, arms crossed.

"What's up?"

I took a breath. "What happened the other day…" I trailed off, remembering Dr. Yao's advice to take other's perspectives. "When I said I wasn't ready now, it didn't mean I wasn't going to be ready soon."

"What?" he asked, raising an eyebrow. "Ready for what?"

"To date you," I filled in, feeling utterly dumb. *Was I speaking in a different language lately?* "I'm not going to be ready… ever."

"I'm confused." Justin stood from his leaning position, looking slightly down at me from his height. I sighed, giving up.

"Why do people think we're dating?

He cocked his head. "People think we're dating?"

"Hampton does!" I exclaimed.

"So let me get this straight," he started, a smile forming.

"You think I've been telling people that you and I are back together?"

"Didn't you?"

"No," he said, blinking. "I didn't." I stared, dumbfounded. Justin put a hand to his heart. "I'd like to think I have a little more self-respect than to go around telling everyone we were back together. You know, considering you've turned me down oh-so-many times."

I hid a smile. "Not that many."

"Are you, uh?" he scratched his head, "into Hampton or something?"

"What makes you think that?"

"You were about to chop my head off because he thought we were together," Justin said.

"Need I say more?"

"I don't know," was all I said, because how was I about to have a conversation with my ex-boyfriend about how I may or may not be interested in someone else? *Can you spell awkward?*

He shrugged, giving me a half-smile. "We don't have to talk about it."

I blew out a tiny breath. *Thank God.*

"But he's a good guy. He freaked on Annie the night of the bonfire. When you, um, left."

"What do you mean?"

"Well," he started, pausing as someone passed us and pushed into the lunchroom doors. "Annie started to laugh about the whole thing and then asked Hampton if he wanted to come to her house for an afterparty. He started to yell at her, asking her why she was such a bitch."

My eyes widened. Hampton called Annie a bitch. "Wow. That's—"

"Crazy that someone finally stood up to her? Especially since he's the new kid."

"I stood up to her. The night of Jack," I said quietly. We'd never talked about the details.

"I know you did," Justin said, his voice softer. I gave him a questioning look.

"Don't you remember?" he asked. "You explained everything to me that night." I gave him a blank stare. I had no idea what he was talking about.

His expression changed. "You told me all about it. At McDonalds." I found myself shaking my head.

"No, I was never with you after it happened. How could I have told you?"

Justin put a hand on my forearm, his thumb rubbing small circles. "I was with you for over an hour. Annie called me and told me to come to where it all happened, and I came and found you. I sat with you for a little bit. You didn't say much, just that you yelled at Annie and were never going to be friends again."

I took a small step backward. "What?" A strange sense fell over me.

How could I seriously not remember?

"Was I that drunk?"

"I mean," he said, pausing.

"You weren't that bad. I had only had a few drinks, but you were pretty conscious."

"Conscious?"

"Again, you didn't say much to me. I kinda just…" he shifted, seeming uncomfortable.

"Held you. And you cried. Then you went silent by the time your parents were alerted."

"Why haven't you told me this before?"

Was he kidding? Dropping all this on me now?

"I assumed you knew. And it's not like you ever let me talk to you." My stomach dropped; here I was, shutting Justin in the dark after a night of comforting me. God, Annie wasn't the bitch. *I was.*

But maybe that's why we were the perfect friends.

"I'm so sorry," I whispered. The warning bell sounded in the distance, and I shot him an apologetic look for missing lunch.

"It's okay; we're talking about it now." Shuffling started to erupt behind the closed doors.

"Have you talked to Annie about any of this?" I gave him, and *are you kidding me?* Face.

"Right, well. I think you should," he said, starting toward the doors to grab his stuff.

"I'll address the 'rumor,' if there even is one." I nodded, Hampton far from my mind.

Did I have to talk to Annie?

Chapter 23

That morning, Dad drove Grandma to the airport and then to my appointment with Dr. Yao. Boy, did I have things to tell her…

"So what you're saying is," Dr. Yao's eyes zeroed in on me, "Justin uncovered a pocket of time in which you have no recollection of?" I sat for a beat, rearranging it into layman's terms.

"Yes." I nodded. "Do you think he's lying?"

"Why would he?"

"Maybe he's trying to make me realize how much he was there for me and that I really do need him in my life when he comforted me so well, to begin with?" Even as I said it, I knew it sounded crazy. And too complex for a seventeen-year-old boy obsessed with soccer and sour patch kids to conjure up.

She looked at me, raising an eyebrow. "I'm not sure. I personally don't think so, but go with your gut." Dr. Yao was all about gut instincts. What did your gut feel during that? Or what about then? She told me that the gut was considered the second brain, lined with one hundred million nerves.

I sat back, a bad feeling churning in my belly. "It's just really unsettling that I don't remember that."

"Not completely surprising," Dr. Yao said. "It was a traumatic experience, and we've already discovered some of your coping mechanisms. You took a big step and confronted Justin, and he recalled events of which you have no remembrance. Do you think this is telling you something?"

I looked at her, a question in my eyes. How was speaking to Justin and finding out about something truly disturbing a good thing for me? But then, I stopped. "No. I can't do that."

"You already did it with Justin," she emphasized to me. "And that's proved to be healing for you. This is obviously one of the harder steps, but I think it needs to be done."

"Why is it necessary? She hates me."

"For the same reason that came out of reconnecting with Justin, do you feel better now that you two have settled the issues and spoken your peace? Do you feel you can say hello to him and not regret it?" Dr. Yao asked.

"Yes," I mumbled. "But Justin still loves me. Annie blames me for it all."

"How do you know?"

I stopped, pausing. I… didn't. The truth was that after the accident, she aggressively ignored me. I'd always assumed it was because I was the one driving and hitting Jack. Was it something else?

"Talking to Annie is one of the last puzzle pieces."

"To what?"

Dr. Yao gave me a soft smile. "Moving on. To free yourself from the guilt that's been hiding deep inside you. To find answers, because it seems like the story isn't what you think it is."

*

I lived through the week of school with a horrible, horrible sense of building dread. I almost wished I could go back and hide under my covers, staring at the tree outside my window and losing myself in the peace it exuded.

But I couldn't because I needed to talk to Annie. It was my last homework assignment, or at least I thought it was. I'd been through over a month of sessions with Dr. Yao and had very few remaining.

"Why do you look like that?"

I looked to my left, straight into Justin's eyes. I scowled. "Nice." Our teacher was experiencing some major technical difficulties, and we had minutes remaining.

"No, I just mean you have a weird look on your face."

"Just thinking," I said, swallowing and watching the clock tick by with the remaining moments of class.

"Is everything okay?" he asked.

"Things are fine."

"Did you talk to Hampton?" I did a double-take.

"What?"

"Hampton. Did you tell him we weren't dating?" He blinked, looking genuinely interested. Justin always wanted me to be happy, right from the moment we met when we were little to offering me his bike to ride back to the neighborhood just so I didn't have to walk. He was always going to be there for me.

"No," I said, looking back at the clock. One minute. "I haven't."

"Well, why not?" I had more pressing matters.

I parted my lips and was about to say that I hadn't seen him when the bell rang.

Shuffling erupted immediately, and Mr. Gento growled in frustration from the front of the room. He tossed the remote at the desk, shaking his head.

"Penny?" I heard Justin calling my name, but I pretended I hadn't heard and left the room. It was lunchtime, the most dreaded part of the day. My feet felt heavier with every step I took with the crowd to the coordinate plane. It was like they moved on autopilot while I was just along for the ride. It's been a while since I felt that way. It spooked me.

Jess caught up to me in line, cutting the freshman behind her. "Why do you look like that?"

"Why is everyone asking me that today?"

"You just look tense. Nervous," she paused, turning to me with wide eyes. She leaned closer to my ear. "Are you planning on talking to Hampton today?"

I shook my head, my chest aching a bit. I wanted to clear that up so badly with him, but Annie had to be dealt with first. "I'll tell you at the table." We got our food and headed to the vacant corner.

"I have to talk to Annie," I blurted out, not able to keep it in any longer. Jess looked at me like I was crazy.

"Why?"

"Homework assignment from the therapist," I said, cracking open my yogurt and taking a spoonful.

"To talk to the girl who's a massive sociopath?"

I shrugged. "You know how I talked to Justin yesterday?"

She nodded. I'd informed her of the gist of it all, but not this.

"Well, he told me more about that night. Stuff I had no idea happened. And then I realized that Annie and I never talked about anything that'd happened. We stopped being friends the moment Jack died."

"I'm not really getting it." She peeled her banana. "You think Annie knows stuff that you don't know? Or just forgot?"

I nodded. Exactly.

"I think it'll be good closure for me," I said, taking a breath. "And if Justin told me about an entire hour I'd forgotten, then who knows what else happened that I don't know of?"

"I guess it'll be good to talk to her," Jess said.

"But if she tries to kill you," she squinted.

"I'm there in a flash to take her down." We laughed, and I felt a little better.

"So, how are you gonna do it?" she asked. "Go up the Mets's table and just ask to talk to her?" I eyed their table. Annie threw her perfect head of blonde hair back, laughing at something Claire said. By the look on Claire's face, Annie's laugh looked more malicious than something they were sharing together. I shuddered. Maybe not.

I took out my phone, scrolled through my texts to the very bottom, and found Annie's name. I hadn't read our texts in months, so it felt weird typing something in the text box.

"Are you texting her?" Jess whisper-yelled. I texted a few messages, shaking my head each time and deleting them.

Finally, I settled on: *Are you busy right now?*

I hit send.

It's not the most brilliant question, but I wanted to get it over with. "Oh, my God. You've gone rogue." She completely abandoned her lunch, grabbing my phone from the table and reading the text.

I watched for Annie's reaction over Jess's head. "Don't turn around. She's reaching for her phone." I watched her pick up her phone and turn it in her hand, her face visibly freezing. She lost the smile she had moments prior and instead was icy. She looked up, meeting my eyes. We held eye contact for a moment—one frigid, airless stare—and then it was gone. Annie turned her phone off, flipped it over, and refocused on her friends. But I could tell she was rattled. She wasn't as attentive to whatever her friends were saying, and I could practically see the question marks behind her eyes.

"She looked at it and didn't respond."

"Bitch," Jess said.

I picked up my phone to text her again: *Can we talk? It's important.*

I hit send and watched her eyes dart to her vibrating phone. Her gaze fell to mine, almost saying, "What's wrong with you?" but she checked it anyway. She read it, flipped it over again, and ignored it. I sighed, pulling myself up and not letting myself think too much about what I was about to do. She was my friend once; why should I be scared of her?

"What are you doing?" Jess asked. My feet moved me to the Westside, right up to Annie's table. Claire, Jasmine, Heather, and Courtney stared up at me, daggers in their eyes. Annie stared at her food, ignoring me.

"What do you think you're doing?" Claire asked, glancing at Annie in a clear attempt to get back on her side.

Annie finally looked at me. "What do you want, *Penelope*?" She emphasized my full name, making it sound long, ugly, and full. I almost laughed, unfazed.

"I know you saw my texts," I said.

"She's texting you?" Heather asked, confused.

"Why is she texting you?"

"Are you friends again?" Jasmine asked.

Courtney laughed. "What the hell is going on?" The commotion had stirred others' attention, including Justin's table. Where Hampton sat. I forced myself not to let my eyes wander toward him.

"Everyone shut up," Annie barked, and the table fell silent. She looked at me. "You don't belong here. Leave." I watched her face, but the way she looked at me at that time was slightly different. We stared at each other, and she gave me the tiniest of tiniest nods. I ripped my eyes away, leaving the table and heading back to the Eastside.

Jess was laughing when I sat down. "Miss Thang, up top!"

She held out her hand for a high five. I gave her a low one.

"Don't get too excited," I said.

"She told me to leave."

"And you listened to her?"

"Just wait," I said, and I watched my phone.

"What are we waiting for?" The screen remained dark, and in a few moments, it lit up from a text.

Annie texted me back, saying, *Tonight at the dock. Eight p.m.*

I passed my phone to Jess, feeling like I'd won. But only a little, because I was talking to Annie in less than a few hours.

Chapter 24

I stood on the boardwalk, squeezing my fingers together. One by one. Thumb, pointer, middle, ring, and pinky. Over and over as I stared at the setting sun hitting the horizon. Fishermen in the distance were docking their boats and transporting the catch of the day to the sidewalk, ready to be sold at the fish market the following morning. On the beach, older couples sat on lawn chairs, watching the setting sun with drinks in their hands. Vacationing families who'd been at the beach for the majority of the day looked tired, throwing dry clothes over their toddlers, gathering scattered toys, and packing up discarded trash and food—all while still trying to catch a peak of the sun. I shifted my footing, checking the time on my phone. It was ten minutes after eight. She was late. *Was she ditching?*

Couples ambled a few feet away from me, holding each other's hands. I didn't recognize anyone, so that was a plus. I'm sure Annie wasn't thrilled about the idea of having Royal High students catch a glimpse of the school's all-time enemies having a private conversation.

My phone buzzed in my hand, and I checked it, half expecting it to be Annie telling me where to stick it, but it was Jess.

The message read, *Do you see her?*

I texted back that she hadn't shown up yet, making a joke about her never coming in the first place and wondering if she enjoyed catfishing people. I pressed send, looking up to Annie.

She was walking down the boardwalk, dressed in black sweats and a matching hoodie, arms crossed tight across her chest. By the time she got to me, I eyed her outfit.

"Camo' much?" I asked.

Annie smiled sweetly. "Wouldn't want anyone I know to see me talking to the town's killer." We were off to a great start. "Why am I here?"

I swallowed. "I have some questions about the night Jack died."

She gave a short laugh that lacked humor. "The night you killed my boyfriend, how could I forget?"

My chest burned in frustration. "This is besides the point, but you were planning on ending it that night. You know what he was to you, so don't pretend that you two were in love." I paused, realizing something.

"Who the hell do you think you are?" she asked.

"Someone who's finally woken up."

Annie rolled her eyes. "Did you ask me here so you could get your revenge from the bonfire? Be a bitch back to make yourself feel better."

I shook my head, my nerves falling away as the conversation continued. I didn't know why I was ever afraid of her; she was the same, insecure girl who I'd once been best friends with. "No, because I'm not a bitch."

"Oh, really?" She raised a perfectly waxed eyebrow. "Do you not recall anything when we were friends? Honestly, Penny, sometimes I even thought you were being a bit harsh." It was true. I was a mean girl. A clone of Annie. But everything changed the night Jack died. I was forced to look at myself in the mirror and recognize the person I'd become. It was part of the reason why I wanted to hide so much; I wasn't sure how I'd let myself get to that point.

I sighed, looking out over the water. "I don't wanna fight."

"Then *why* am I here?" Annie repeated herself, taking a step closer. I looked at her and for a moment, I was sure I'd seen a flash of fear. *What did she have to be afraid of?*

"I was talking to Justin the other day, and we got into talking about Jack. He told me the whole story of him coming to us and me crying to him. Do you remember him showing up to McDonald's?"

Annie stared at me, the same flash of fear running through her face. It was gone in an instant, and she regained her initial stoic face. "Yeah, he did. But only for, like, fifteen minutes. Then you told him to leave."

Fifteen minutes?

"He said he was there for an hour with me," I said, my brows drawing together.

"Oh," she said lamely, shrugging and looking at the setting sun. It cast a warm shadow on her face, dipping fast over the horizon.

It'd be dark in a few minutes.

"I guess," I started. "I've just realized we've never talked about anything that happened, and I wanted to know if there's anything I don't remember."

"Why do we need to even talk about it?" she asked, her tone cold and clipped. "What's the point in that? Jack's dead. End of story."

I found myself shaking my head. "There are holes in the story."

"But there aren't," she urged.

"Can't we just talk about it?"

"We don't need to revisit any of this." Annie was breaking,

tears forming in her eyes. She started to turn away. "This is bullshit."

I grabbed her, and she whipped around, pushing me off her. "Don't touch me!" I stepped close to her, searching her face. That time, I was sure of it; Annie was scared. *Really scared.*

"What don't I know?" I whispered.

Annie's lip trembled, her breathing increasing at a rapid pace. I wasn't sure how long we'd stood there for until she looked to the side, took a deep breath, and met my eyes. When she spoke, it was so low of a whisper that I almost asked her to repeat herself. But I heard her say, "I was driving."

I stared, wondering if I'd even heard her right. But judging by the look on her face, I knew what she'd said. I took a staggering step backward, feeling like I was living a fever dream. "What?"

"I was driving," she said, her voice more steady. But just a little.

"I *heard* you," I seethed, tears beginning to stream down my face. "I'm wondering what the hell that means."

She stared without a word, her flat expression unmoving. "We got in the car at Eric's, and at that point, you were driving. Everything was fine, until we got to McDonald's. We started fighting, and Jack was pretty drunk. He threw up all outside of the car." So far, it was everything I already knew.

So then, how did we switch seats?

"I wanted to play music, and you said no because we were all buzzed, and it wasn't safe." Her tone quivered, and she continued. "And then you told me that if I wanted to play music, then you weren't going to be the one driving."

What?

"Why don't I remember this?" I heard myself asking. But

she continued without a hitch.

"You got out of the car, and we were still yelling at each other. We switched seats, and I," Annie paused, "started to play music. Pretty loud, just so I could shove it in your face." She noticeably paused, swallowing what looked like a hard lump.

"I didn't hear the back door open when Jack got out." She started shaking her head, and tears started to stream down her cheeks. "Why did he get out of the car in the first place? Everything would have been fine if he'd just eaten the food in the back." I couldn't believe what I was watching; Annie was a mess. Her mascara started to drip.

A tear of my own bounced off my cheek, hitting the boardwalk beneath us. "What happened next?"

Annie swallowed, closing her eyes. "I started the car, and you screamed. Something about stopping the car… I guess you saw him before I did." The sounds of the lapping waves filled the heavy silence between us.

"And then I got out of the car," I said, filling in the next point. "And you didn't move."

Her head whipped around to mine. "No, Penny. I was the one who got out. You didn't move. You were paralyzed. I kept screaming at you to get out of the car and help, but you just stared." Something still didn't make sense.

"Why did I think that I was driving?" It was the longest she took to respond, and she avoided my eye contact.

I said, "Annie. Why did I think I was driving?"

"Because I told everyone you were the one who hit him." Her face was a wreck; her eyes and nose were rimmed in red, and her makeup was wiped clean by her secrets.

"Including you."

I stared at a girl whom I once called my best friend, blinking once. Twice. Three times.

"The police and ambulance came, and they asked me what happened. I'd gotten you out of the car at that point, but you sat on the curb and just stared at Jack on the ground."

Annie pressed her lips together. "You made it easy for me to lie."

"To manipulate me," I whispered, correcting her.

She considered my choice of words, eventually giving a defeated, slight nod.

"How could you do that to me?" I asked.

"I'm sorry," she said. "It was freaking me out, and I was thinking that it would ruin my life. Or that they'd throw me in jail, and I'd never go to college or get out of this stupid town."

"So you thought it was okay that my life would be ruined?" I asked, angry. "*How could you do that to me?*"

"It was like you had short-term memory loss or something," Annie said, shaking her head. "I was yelling at you to get out of the car, and you didn't budge. I had to force you out. You sat on the curb and asked me what *happened*. I was so confused."

"So, instead of explaining the truth, you told me that I was the one driving?" I yelled. "Are you crazy? What is wrong with you?"

"Jack's family didn't press charges," she said, thinking it would make it better. "They let it go and knew it was a horrible, horrible accident."

"No," I said. "It was only an accident because you were being a bitch, as usual, and weren't paying attention!"

"This wasn't all my fault." Annie turned away from me; the sun had already set. It was dark.

"Oh, classic Annie. Nothing's ever your fault, right?"

She turned to me, crossing her arms. "That's not what I

said."

"So then, why were you so awful to me after? Let me have no friends. Throw me to the Eastside."

She was quiet. The darkness almost gave me more room to explode on her. "I had to keep the story going."

"I'm telling everyone," I said, walking away from her.

She grabbed my arm, pulling me back. "Penny, don't. You'll look crazy." I stopped. "You know I have more power. People will believe me over you, and you know it." She was right.

So right.

"The only person that really knows what happened was Jack, and he's gone."

I was trapped.

"We're graduating," Annie shrugged. "Who cares what these people think?"

"Says the girl who made up this *bullshit* just so people wouldn't turn on her," I said. "You're out of your mind."

"*No one* will believe you," she said again, sounding scared once more. "Can we just put this behind us?"

I felt a presence behind me, and I instantly felt better knowing who it was.

Jess herself, dressed in black leggings and a hot pink hoodie, appeared, grinning. "I always knew you were a psychotic bitch. Can't say I'm surprised you'd do something like this." When Jess read the texts earlier today, we'd conspired to have her stand nearby and listen in. I'd never been so happy to have someone by my side.

Annie's face, even in the dark, turned stark white. "What the hell is this?"

"I was standing over there the whole time," Jess said, pointing to where her spot was. "You didn't think I'd let Penny come to this alone, would you?"

"You freaks deserve each other," Annie said, looking between the two of us. Jess started to step forward, but I pulled her back.

"Do you know what you put me through?" I asked. "And you didn't feel guilty?" I watched her take a steadying breath.

"I did. But I figured you'd be okay with Justin and everything. It's not my fault you broke the poor boy's heart."

"No, it's not," I said, shaking my head. "But you sure made it easier."

She looked down. "Well, you have Hampton now. The boy's crazy for you." My heart warmed for just a moment but was pulled back into reality. The twisted reality that Annie created for me. The one where I lost myself in being a mean girl, going too far with it, and making bad decisions along the way. No, it wasn't all Annie's fault.

I messed up, too. But it was time I took my life back.

I looked at Jess. "Let's go."

She nodded, and together, we left Annie alone on the boardwalk.

Chapter 25

Thanksgiving was looming, which meant Grandma was planning to make her way back to us. Grandma called me a few days a week, giving me updates on how she finally managed to snag the neighbor but also asking me how things were going with market-boy. She meant Hampton but swore she could "never remember his name but knew it sounded exotic." I wouldn't necessarily describe his name as such, but Grandma was Grandma.

Besides Jess, I hadn't told a soul about the secrets that Annie unleashed. Jess had been practically bouncing out of her seat when we started to drive away, thinking about the way Royal High was going to turn on their Queen Bee when I stopped her.

"I don't know if I'm going to say anything," I said, looking out the dark window.

There was a brief moment of silence before she started to laugh.

I looked at her. "What?"

"That's funny, Penny," she grinned, turning on her blinker as she pulled into the left lane, stopping the car for a red light.

"I'm being serious."

Jess's head whipped to mine, her ponytail swishing. "What are you even talking about?"

I shrugged. "What would it gain? Yeah, I feel a little better, but I think I need some time myself to think about what Annie just told me." Jess was quiet but listening.

"Just give me some time, and then we'll figure out what to

do." Okay, I'll admit, it was a half-lie. Yes, it was true that I needed some time to debrief a memory I had assumed was so correct for months when, in actuality, it was so false. While a small weight of relief was lifted from my shoulders, a pain still existed in the Jack-sized hole left in my chest. So with that, I bought myself some time to figure out what I was going to do. I wasn't planning on actively doing something with the information I'd learned; it all had become too messy and tangled. And lately, when anything was suddenly too difficult to understand myself, I brought it to the one person who had a degree in solving dilemmas. That's how I saw it, at least.

On the last day of school, I sat across from Dr. Yao in the afternoon. I'd rode my bike straight from Royal High, and Shirley was parked—in all her purple and white glory—outside the office.

"So, what do you think about all this?" Her face had been interestingly calm throughout the juicy story.

I shrugged. "I wasn't planning on telling anyone."

"Why?"

"Because," I paused. "I don't feel necessarily better that I know I wasn't the one driving. I mean, at first I did. But I had some time to think about it, and I'm thinking that there's a shared responsibility between the two of us. Regardless of who was driving the car."

She nodded, seeming impressed with my dissection. I guess I was, too. "Does Annie know you're not planning on telling anyone?"

I hid a smile. "No."

Dr. Yao nodded slowly, a small smile of her own creeping forward. "I'm really proud of the fact that you texted Annie and made the step to meet with her."

"She just seemed really afraid," I said, thinking. I shrugged. "I felt kinda bad." At that moment, she closed her book and crossed her legs. It unsettled me because there was never a moment when she didn't have her legs crossed, and the book opened.

"I think we can end early today," was all she said, peering at me. My face paled.

Did I do something wrong? Say something wrong?

"You didn't do anything wrong, Penny."

And just like that, Dr. Yao read my mind once again. "This is a good thing. You've made huge progress."

I straightened. "Really?"

"Five weeks ago, did you ever think you would feel *bad* for Annie?"

I shrugged. "I guess not."

She nodded in response and, after a brief moment of silence, said, "I'll see you in two weeks. Enjoy the break with your family."

I wanted to say, "Wait, tell me what I'm missing," but she was up and crossing the room to the desk before I could even think of speaking. She started scribbling something on a notepad, ripping the page from the pad, and handing it to me. It was the date and time of my next appointment.

"Have a good Thanksgiving, Penny." She smiled, it being my cue to leave. Twenty minutes early. And with that, I left Dr. Yao's office with a little bit of confusion mixed with thoughts of our Thanksgiving meal.

*

"Potatoes, cranberries, green beans, cornbread mix, dinner rolls, veggies for salad, broccoli casserole…" Mom listed off the shopping list to Dad and I, making sure nothing was forgotten from the paper slip gripped in her hand. "Did I miss something?"

"The turkey?" I asked, smiling. Before, I would've been snarky about it. But Mom and I's relationship was getting better and better every day, inch by inch.

"Oh! Right, right," Mom said, scribbling it down. "Should I get a ham, too? I'll get a ham." I peered closer at her; she was noticeably antsy. Hair strands falling from her usually perfect ponytail. Thanksgiving was usually a big holiday at my house, and Mom almost always went all out with the food and decor, but this time was different.

"Why are you acting weird?"

"Weird?" Mom questioned me, inspecting the list again. "I'm not acting weird." Dad chuckled nearby.

"Are you seeing what I'm seeing?" I asked Dad.

He poured himself a cup of coffee. "She just wants everything to be perfect, considering the company is coming."

"Company?" I asked, grinning and poking the beast. "Since when do you want to impress Grandma? That's why we're getting enough food for Port Royal?"

Mom sighed, eyes meeting Dad's. They held eye contact for a moment, shared a sigh, and locked eyes with mine.

"What's going on?" They both continued to stare calmly, blinking a few times.

Mom with her pursed lips. Dad with his nervous tick of sipping coffee.

"I ran into Annie's mom a few days ago," Mom started, putting down her list. "And, well, there's some pretty tough family stuff going on right now with them."

"Like what?"

"With Roger," she explained. "Annie's dad? You remember—?"

"I remember," I said. I'd only known Annie's dad to be a robotic figure; lots of "Hi, honey-bunny" and "see ya later, alligator's." Nothing more, nothing less. I remember always feeling extra grateful for my dad and what he was, giving him an extra tighter squeeze when he would pick me up from sleepovers and playdates.

"What does this have to do with anything?"

Another sigh. Two sighs, actually, from both Mom and Dad. Another sip of coffee from Dad. More pursing of lips from Mom. "I invited both Annie and her mother to Thanksgiving dinner," Mom said, her eyes prepared to take my wrath.

"What?" I stood, looking between the two. My eyes bulged. "What?" I slid off the kitchen stool in an instant, the hardwood floors beneath me creaking under my weight. "Is this a joke?"

"Their family situation is… sad, and we always have more than enough food on Thanksgiving. One thing led to another, and I invited her."

If Mom only knew what she did to me, I thought of telling her. And Dad. But what would it even do? Other than rehashing the most awful day of my life so far, only to get even more mad at something we can't fix.

"She hates me. Actually, they *both* hate me," I said, point blank.

"And now that I think about it, do *you* hate me?"

"Oh, Penny," Mom's head tilted. "You know that's not true."

Which part, exactly?

Because I was pretty clear on about seventy-five percent of it.

"It's only for a few hours, Pen," Dad, for good measure,

piped up. "You don't even have to sit next to each other. You can hang out with Grandma!"

"I can't believe I'm having this conversation." I crossed my arms, looking past the both of them. My favorite tree's branches swayed outside in the chilly wind.

Mom was at my side, moving a stray strand of hair off my cheek. "They're having a tough time right now." *What did that even mean?* Since when did Annie have 'tough times'? "I don't want you to think I'm betraying you."

I snorted. "Aren't you?"

"It's just a meal," Mom said. "You can even invite Jess if you want."

"There you go!" Dad exclaimed, tipping his cup at me. I wanted to glare at him, but I couldn't. Because all I saw was the ever-present golden retriever. Who could be mean to a soft and happy dog?

"We're going to have to pull even more chairs out to fit nine guests." Nine? I wasn't great at math (read: I was horrible), but I didn't think that Annie, her mom, and Jess even added up to that.

Mom's head whipped to his, eyes widening. "John. Really?"

I retook my seat on the bar stool, feeling a bit dizzy from the amount of surprises. "Who else is coming? The Mets? Let's make it an 'I-Hate-Penny party'."

Mom rolled her eyes. "You know the Prescotts, right?"

My stomach plummeted. All the way to the depths of hell. Frozen, I managed a nod. "I've been going on walks with Jane." His mother.

"Since when do you walk?"

She ignored me. "They're new in town and don't know many people yet, and thought since I'd already invited Mrs. Prickett, I'd invite them too."

"Them?" I held my breath, waiting for what I already knew

was going to come. Mom nodded. "Jane and her two sons, Hampton and Jayden, you already know Hampton, right? It'll be fun."

Chapter 26

"This is a tragedy," I said to Jess, who was busy applying her own makeup in the mirror. "Annie and *her mother* are about to be here."

She grinned at my dramatics, looking at me through the mirror. The guests would be arriving in thirty minutes, and the smell of Thanksgiving foods wafted through the house and up the stairs. Jess, thank *God*, was able to get out of her own Thanksgiving for my own personal night of hell. It was *very* uncharacteristic of her family to allow her to skip out on family events, but Jess must've made quite the argument: that I *was* family, and I needed her support.

"I think it's great," she said.

I put a pillow over my head, considering suffocating myself. "I'm going to pretend you didn't just say that."

Jess curled her eyelashes with the mascara wand. "Ever since she admitted she brainwashed you, you know she'll be walking on eggshells all night. You have the power right now."

"I don't want the power," I said glumly, resting my chin in my hand. "I just want to graduate."

"Want me to do your hair?" Jess held up the iron, wiggling her eyebrows. "Royal High's favorite boy is about to be in your living room."

"That's another thing. What am I supposed to say to him?" I resisted the urge to burrow my head into my pillow, not wanting to ruin my makeup.

"That you're really into him?" It came out like a question, in an, *um, duh?* Sorta way. "She started counting on her fingers: "That you don't have a boyfriend like he thought you did, the message on those gross potato chips was heard loud and clear, and oh, you want to kiss his face off?"

"Okay, I get it," I said, shaking my head.

"There are so many things to say to him. What's the holdup?" She asked seriously this time, plugging in the iron and setting it on the vanity.

"I don't know," I said. "I think—I think I'm…"

"Nervous?" Jess filled in while I surrendered with a nod. "It's totally normal to be nervous. You haven't been with a guy since the accident with Jack, and just like talking to Annie was one of the tasks that Dr. Yao gave you, letting yourself get back out there and tell a guy how you feel is one of them, too."

"Since when did you get your PhD?" I grinned.

"On the weekends in my free time," Jess gave a nonchalant shrug, feeling the iron for its level of heat. "Plus, I can finally submit my art portfolio to Parsons if you talk to him."

I threw the pillow in my hand at her. "Shut up! You're lying."

"I'm not!" She giggled, dodging the pillow. "A deal was a deal."

"Okay, one: I already talked to him," I said, holding up a finger, "and two: I told you that you were crazy for doing that."

"Calm yourself, Penelope." She rolled her eyes. "Of course, I submitted my portfolio."

I sighed. "Good."

"The morning after I heard about your bathroom date with Hampton."

Jess grinned. "What exactly happened in that bathroom?

Any details mysteriously left out?"

I thought back, remembering the short distance between Hampton and me in that four-by-four bathroom, his face so close that I could see the tiny freckle above his lips…. my face grew red. I brought my hands to my warm neck. "No, we didn't do anything. I walked in on him peeing."

"I didn't know you were kinky like that."

I scowled, standing and crossing the room. "Do my hair."

"Boss-y," she said, but went to work anyway, separating my hair into sections, then straightening pieces.

"Do I just go out and say it?" I asked.

"Say what?" A piece of straightened hair was moved to my shoulder.

I huffed, irritated that she was making me say it. "That I like him."

"Aha!" Jess cheered, stepping away from my hair with the wand in her hand. She danced in a circle, arms above her head. The wire got caught in her legs, and she had to readjust her footing. "Finally! It took you long enough."

Just then, we heard Dad yell up to us. "What are you ladies doing? You've been in that room for ages."

Grandma, just as loudly, replied, "Never rush a girl! Especially when market-boy is coming."

"Market-boy," Jess repeated, looking at me. "Does she mean Hampton?"

I took a breath, trying to settle the rising nausea in my tummy. "Is it too late to go to your house?" The doorbell rang downstairs, ricocheting through the house and into the core of my bones.

"Now it is," Jess said. "Turn. So I can finish your hair." By the time we got into the kitchen—hair, makeup, and outfits all done—I tried to channel the energy I used to take with me when I flirted with boys. But as hard as I searched, it couldn't be found.

Hampton and his family were standing in the front hall, but no sign of Annie and her mother just yet. My eyes went straight to Hampton, who smiled politely at something my mom said. His mom stood next to him, motioning to Hampton's little brother, who stood meekly and stared down at a phone in his hands. I kept a soft smile, watching him and remembering what Hampton said about him being on the edge of the spectrum. He looked like a mini version of Hampton, just… less social. But the same dirty blonde hair. The same tanned skin. The same green-hazel eyes. The only thing that was really different was their jaws; Hampton's was sharper and more mature, whereas Jayden's was more kiddish. Still developing.

"Penny! Come over here and say hello," Mom said, beckoning me over. She tried to give me her best nonchalant wink, but it looked like she was scrunching her face and had an itch she couldn't quite reach.

I'd made an effort recently to warm up to her; after she gave the news that the Prescotts would be joining us, I wanted so badly to talk to Jess about the nightmare, but she was busy doing something with her family. After sitting in my room for what felt like ages, I finally got the courage to venture downstairs and ask Mom for some advice, or really, to have someone to listen to my rants. Her eyes lit up, and over steaming cups of Earl Grey tea, I mentioned my developing crush on the new kid in town. She acted very cool and unfazed, but I could tell she was squirming on the inside. To yell and jump and give a happy dance for having a conversation so familiar and recognizable with her daughter. But she kept it subdued and actually gave some pretty good, Mom-approved advice on how to talk to him. I'd put the cups in the sink, rinsing them and thinking Mom and I were off to a good start at repairing our relationship.

I reached the Prescotts. "It's nice to see you again!" Mrs. Prescott said. She smiled a genuine smile, reaching out to give me a hug. She smelled of Chanel.

Hampton gave me a smile, too—a smile so warm, nice, and cute that I wanted to scream in his face right then and there and say, "I'm single! I'm not with Justin!" But of course, with a pinch from Jess to remind me to respond, I smiled back and spoke to his mother.

"Hi, Mrs. Prescott," I said. "How are you liking Port Royal so far?" I mostly tuned out her response, which had something to do with loving the 'quaint' town as well as all the nice people she'd met so far. It continued that way for a little bit longer, with more polite nodding and embellished exclamatory remarks on my end before Grandma interjected.

"So you two have met?" She clasped her hands together, looking between myself and Hampton's mother. I knew what she was hinting toward, remembering one of her tips she tossed out in the open one night: "Now, Penny, one of the most important relationships you can have is with your husband's mother. If she doesn't like you and he doesn't have enough balls, you're out."

I asked her, "But what if he does have balls?"

To which she answered, "Then it'll be a pretty tough time. The mothers of boys are," she hovered her pointer finger, twirling it to her temple.

"Trust me, I would know." I grinned, wondering how crazy Grandma must have been with all of Dad's girlfriends. I made a mental note to ask him.

That day, Grandma was sporting a butterfly-covered ribbon, and it would have been super cute if the butterflies weren't a zebra print.

Mrs. Prescott said, "We met Penny when Hampton and I were touring Royal High. She was his shadow buddy."

"Shadow-buddy," Grandma not-so-subtly wiggled her eyebrows at me, and I swear I wanted to exit the room as fast as I'd entered it.

"Sounds... friendly. You didn't tell me that, Penelope." Out of all the adjectives in the English language, couldn't she have picked something other than 'friendly'?

"I'm a tour guide, so I give them all the time," I lied, shrugging and catching eyes with Hampton.

"Wasn't *that* important," something flashed across his face, but it was gone before I could decipher it.

God, I could kick myself. 'Wasn't that important.' Great flirting, Penny.

Dad jumped in, saving me from any further conversation. "How about we go into the living room? Would you like a drink, Mrs. Prescott?" And off the adults went; Jess threw me a look over her shoulder as she followed my mom, and I could practically see the thumbs-up in her pupils.

I was alone with Hampton.

"Happy Thanksgiving," Hampton said, his voice scratchy and *so*, so hot. "Thanks for inviting us."

"Thank my mom; it was all her doing. I didn't even know about it." As soon as it left my mouth, I wanted to take back the way it sounded. *God, I was the worst.*

"Oh," he said. "Well, my mom can't cook, so our Thanksgiving is usually an order-in type of night."

"Does your dad cook?"

Hampton shook his head, a moment of pause between us. We'd never talked about his dad, so I wasn't sure why I chose that moment to bring it up. Again, I was the worst. "That's a story for another time." I nodded, unsure how to respond.

"I hope my being here doesn't make Justin uncomfortable," he said, changing the subject. My stomach lurched at the perfect opportunity God laid out for me.

"Speaking of," I started. "That's something I've been meaning to talk to you about." He waited, probably confused.

"I'm not dating Justin. I'm not dating anyone."

"You aren't?" he asked, raising an eyebrow. I shook my head. He responded with a small smile, one similar to the way he used to smile at me before all of our mess.

"I guess your grandma's comments make sense now."

I put a hand around my neck, willing to cover the flush. "I'm sorry for that."

"Don't be." He laughed. "I like her."

I took a breath, needing oxygen for what I was about to say. "Thank you for the chips. I already ate them all."

"Didn't you save any for anyone else?" He laughed.

"Nope," I shook my head, a laugh hiding in my voice. "They're kinda a popular snack in my house. My dad would've eaten the whole bag if he saw them."

"Well," he said, an awkward pause filtering between us. "I'm glad you liked them."

This was it. I channeled the fluttery feeling I got when I read his boyish, handwritten note attached to the bag. "Does the message still stand?"

A look of semi-relief passed over his perfect, perfect face. Hampton looked behind his shoulder, taking a tiny step closer to me. "Do you wanna know a secret?" I instantly thought back to Eric's party, where Hampton and I talked about the power of a good secret.

I nodded, mouth dry.

"It's been standing for a while."

Butterflies flew around my stomach, up my throat, and to my head. I smiled, too nervous to conjure up a good enough response. My eyes wandered to his lips; if I just leaned in…

"Is that okay with you?" he asked, and if we were in a more private environment and he could step closer, I knew he would.

"Yeah," I said. "I think that's very okay with me."

Just then, the front door opened, and the tension between us dropped as Hampton blinked at the door. "Did you know Annie was coming?" At the mention of her name, the butterflies escaped from my tummy and out the kitchen window, left ajar.

*

Jess retreated back to the kitchen to talk to my dad, so I couldn't use her as a buffer. Annie and her mom sat in our living room, where my mom hosted the majority of their own private conversation, while I just stared at her. Annie Prickett was in my living room, taking tiny sips from one of our glasses. Sitting on our couch. Smiling at something my mom said.

I wanted to lunge across the room and tackle her.

But feeling Hampton beside me, I kept calm. His leg was inches from mine, my heart doing flip-flops and cartwheels, and it took all of me to not close the space between us. Instead, I took a breath and looked at his brother in front of us. He was still staring at his phone, headphones having graduated from his head to his neck.

"Jayden, do you like Royal Middle?"

Jayden looked at me, his face frozen in what I thought was fear. Or confusion. His body was tense; his small shoulders were raised, his hands gripping the phone so hard that his knuckles were white, and his feet wrapped around themselves, the tips of his Nike's barely skimming the carpet. "Yeah."

"What do you like about it?" I felt like my nagging parents when they wanted to get something out of me. But it was something to distract me from Annie and her mother in my peripheral vision.

Jayden shrugged, dropping his gaze to his phone. When it was clear he wasn't going to give me any more details, Hampton jumped in to save the day. "He likes his math class. Right, Jayden?"

Jayden looked to his big brother this time, nodding more feverishly. "Yeah, and um," he paused, glancing quickly at me before returning back to his phone, "I like math. It makes the most sense."

I shook my head. "I'm the worst at math. English is my forté."

"English is all right," he mumbled, refusing to make eye contact. "Science is my second favorite."

"Any science in particular?" I asked, shifting on the couch.

"Biology," Jayden said. He tapped away on his phone.

"Biology is cool." I nodded. "I did it freshman year and then never again."

"I remember biology," Hampton said, and his eyes were soft when he looked at me. "I could never forget learning it. My teacher always walked around the class barefoot."

"Eww!" I laughed. "Tell me he had socks on."

He shook his head. "Nope. Barefoot." We laughed together, and I think Jayden's frown had turned slightly upward to make a small smile. Just then, Grandma came into the room with a glass and a fork.

If she was going to do what I thought, she tapped the fork to the glass, clinging, filling the room, and interrupting the light conversation.

"Dinner is served!" she grinned, eyes flitting to Hampton and I. If she could wink at me, I knew she would.

Let torture commenced. By the time we piled our plates and filed to the table, I eyed the seating arrangement.

Hampton automatically took the seat to my left; Jayden was next to him, with Annie literally across from me, sandwiched by Mrs. Prickett and my mom. Hampton's mom sat in their line, beside my mom. My dad and grandma took the two opposing heads, and Jess topped it off by snagging the seat to my right. Earlier that week, Dad went into the basement to find some extra seats.

"Let's give thanks," Grandma said, offering her two hands to Jess and Mrs. Prickett. We all followed suit. Hampton reached for my hand, taking mine in his and giving a squeeze. It enveloped mine completely, making me realize how small my hands really were.

Jess squeezed my other hand, but in a way that said, "Oh my god, he's holding your hand. This is amazing."

"Thank you, Lord, for all the friends we have sitting around this table," Grandma said, her head bowed and eyes closed. I glanced at Annie, who stared at her plate. "We give thanks for all this yummy food we're about to eat and the many blessings we have in our lives. In Jesus's name, I pray, Amen." All hands were dropped, but Hampton held onto mine for a second longer. I bit my tongue to keep from giggling or smiling and started on the mashed potatoes.

The only sound audible was the scraping of forks against the China plates. Annie looked like she wanted to be anywhere but there.

"So, Annie, what are your college plans?" Mom asked.

Her face turned pink, and she noticeably took her time swallowing. "Oh, just a few around Port Royal. I don't wanna go too far." My head shot up from my mashed potatoes. That was all Annie ever wanted to do. Get as far away from this town as possible. What changed?

"Which ones? I went to Clemson, you know." Dad bit some green beans off his fork, looking genuinely interested.

Annie's face was getting a shade redder by the minute. "I think I'm actually going to take a gap year." I almost dropped my fork.

"Oh, that's nice." Dad tried to act nonchalant, but he knew as much as I did that Annie wanted to leave Port Royal and never return. "Where are you planning on going during your gap year?"

"I haven't figured all the details out yet." She smiled, going back to her turkey.

Conversation closed. Mrs. Prickett was oddly quiet throughout the entire conversation. "I took a gap year," Hampton's mom said.

"It was very cool."

"I didn't know that," Hampton said.

"Yeah, well, I wasn't ready to go to college. Part of me was still stuck in high school." I thought of Annie and the irony in that, snorting loudly. Everyone looked at me, and I covered my mouth in horror with my free hand.

Had I seriously just done that?

It was my turn for my face to go red. "Sorry, I had something stuck in my throat." I coughed for emphasis, and everyone regained their conversation about gap years and going abroad. I could feel Annie's stare, and considering it was my house, my food, and my dining room table, I looked at her square in the face. We held eye contact, and she knew my snort was directed at her.

Jess poked my leg, breaking me out of my staring contest. Her voice was just above a whisper. "You okay?" I nodded back.

"Jess," Mrs. Prickett jumped in. "Where are you headed for school?" *Random.*

"Um," she started, smiling. "I actually got an early acceptance letter yesterday. Parsons."

I whipped my head at her so fast, giving me whiplash. "You didn't tell me that!" Cheers erupted from the table, and even Annie managed to give a small smile.

Everyone knew how talented Jess was, even Annie.

"I forgot," she said, giving a tiny shrug and smile. No, Jess didn't forget. My boy problems were taking over most of the conversations lately. I thought for a beat, trying to remember the last time we talked about her.

I pulled her into a hug beside me, whispering in her ear, "Liar." I pulled back. "We're celebrating later."

"Congrats," Hampton said, giving a genuine smile.

"That's awesome. I didn't know you were an artist." I stopped. Was I that bad of a friend that I didn't even mention my best friend being an artist? I drew into myself, contemplating my life and how I'd managed to be such a bad, self-absorbed friend. The doorbell rang. Everyone's chatter was minimized as we all looked at the front door.

My dad rose from the table, dropping his napkin on his seat. "Excuse me, everyone. Please get back to your meals!" He threw his same golden retriever smile at us all, heading toward the door. It rang again, this time sounding more urgent. Everyone fell back into a low chatter, some laughs erupting between mine and Hampton's mom. Maybe this dinner wasn't so bad.

"Hey," Hampton said to me, one of his hands resting on my knee beneath the table. "I found a pretty cool spot I've been wanting to take you to. Want to go later tonight?"

I gave a nod, parting my lips and beginning to say that I would love to, perhaps adding in some cute, flirty comment, when yelling rang through the door and interrupted us all.

"Honey, please listen to me. Let's go!" A male's voice sounded, and everyone's attention at the table turned to the door. Dad looked slightly uncomfortable, unsure of how to handle the rising situation.

"No. I want to give this *nice* family a pie on this *wonderful* holiday. A holiday that Jack couldn't have," a woman's voice said.

I froze. Annie and I locked eyes, and for the first time in a while, we shared the same thought: *Oh my God, that's Jack's mom.*

"Is that who I think it is?" Jess asked, grabbing my arm. I nodded, feeling myself rise from the table like my dad had done moments earlier.

"Who is that?" Hampton asked.

"Penny, don't," both Jess and Annie said at the same time, but I didn't listen. I crossed the room to the front door, opening it further and revealing myself to Jack's parents. Mr. Doe looked tired and stressed but, most of all, humiliated. Dark circles accented his eyes, and the tips of his hair were graying. His wife, Jack's mom, looked anything but put together. She still had a cooking apron on, stained with orange smears and flour. She held a pumpkin pie. Her brown hair frizzed outward, some of it clinging to her neck. The same dark circles accented her eyes as well, but they were rimmed red. Her face was stark white.

"Mrs. Doe—" I started, but Dad stepped in front of me.

"Penny, go sit down," he said in a warning tone, but I didn't care. The last time she saw me was at Moe's with Hampton; the time before that was when I was numb and mute in the driveway of McDonald's, and even then, I wasn't sure if that was a true memory. I didn't go to his funeral. I wouldn't have been welcomed.

"Thanksgiving was Jack's favorite holiday. Did you know that?" That time, she was talking to me, dead in the eyes. Her hazel eyes appeared dark and hollow, sad and angry.

In a knee-jerk reaction, I shook my head in response. No, I didn't know.

"He loved pumpkin pie." She looked down at the pie, cradling it in her arms. Her lip began to tremble. "I think it's only fair that *you* get to eat his favorite pie on this day." The bite in her words took me back, chills erupting over my skin.

"Sweetie, we need to leave these people alone." Mr. Doe placed his hands around his wife's sides. He looked at my dad. "I'm so sorry for this."

My dad stood there, stunned into silence, as he watched the train wreck. Nevertheless, my dad, being my dad, said, "It's okay. I understand."

"*You* understand?" Mrs. Doe asked, laughing a loud laugh. "That's rich. It looks like your daughter is still standing here to this day." I eyed the pumpkin pie in her hand, and the cracks in the center signaled that it hadn't been cooled properly. Like she'd messily baked and retrieved it from the oven with no time to stop and think.

Suddenly, Annie appeared by my side. I looked at her, and it was the first time I felt like we were a team in this horrible, horrible accident.

"Oh, the *other* one!" Mrs. Doe cried. When Annie was

hooking up with boys, she had a strict 'no-parent' rule. No parents were to be met. No attachment was to be made. By the looks of it, Mrs. Doe didn't know Annie's involvement with her son.

Annie parted her lips to say something, frozen.

Mrs. Doe's eyes were wide and blinking fast, tears beginning to stream down her cheeks. Her unmanicured hands gripped the pie dish, trembling.

"Here," she handed it to me, her outstretched arm crossed through our front door. "Enjoy the pie." My hands shook by my sides.

I tried to breathe and remain calm. *Breathe in, breathe out, in four, out eight.*

Her face tightened. She grew visibly angry. "You don't want it?"

"I'll take it," Annie's hands outstretched. Her voice is small. "Thank you."

"No, no." Jack's mother shook her head, a wicked smile growing. "I made this for Penny. The girl who killed my son." The air rushed out of the room. My chest tightened.

"Are you going to take it or not?" she asked, staring me down. "You've taken other things from me with no problem."

Dad said something, moving around us to shut the door.

"I... I—" I started but stopped when she raised the pie high above her head and slammed it into the ground. I jumped, the glass dish shattering. Shards and pumpkin puree covered our front steps and, in an exceedingly dark and twisted comparison, reminded me of the fallen chicken nuggets amongst Jack's splattered blood. Mrs. Doe started sobbing, and I couldn't believe my eyes. Her husband shot an extremely apologetic glance at us, muttering something about coming back later to clean up the mess, when my dad shook his head, saying there was no need, and shut the door.

The silence in the house was deafening. I could feel Hampton's eyes on me.

"I'm gonna get a bag," I heard myself say. "Clean up the mess." Dad put a hand on my back, telling me not to worry about it. Humiliation cursed through me, and it took all of my energy to muster composure and head back to the table. Annie walked with me. I settled into the chair, taking a long sip from my glass of water. Jess put a hand on my arm. The guests stared, and my mother did the same into her lap.

"I'm sorry about that," Dad announced, a certain sadness enveloping his face. "I had... no idea."

"Well," Grandma started. "You should have told her we already had pumpkin pie."

Her comment offered an immense amount of relief to the room, and some smiles broke the icy film of awkwardness.

"Please eat," Mom said, waving her hands. Her cheeks were red, and I could tell she was embarrassed. "Let's not let that ruin our evening."

"Are you okay?" Hampton said it low and quiet, so only I could hear. I could feel my dad's eyes on me, probably checking to make sure I didn't break and shatter like the pie dish. I nodded, reaching for Dad's glass of champagne. He didn't object. I took a sip, the bubbles warming my tummy and doing their job of numbing my nerves. I hadn't had alcohol since the bonfire, but I felt like I'd made enough progress with Dr. Yao that a sip of champagne wouldn't hurt. I could feel Jess's worried gaze on me. I glanced at Annie and her mother; their heads were bent to their meal, murmuring to each other about something.

Mrs. Prescott, frozen in thought, said, "Was that the mother of the boy who died?"

"Mom," Hampton said, piercing the air. He shook his head at her, his hand finding my knee again.

"Yes. He was a student at Royal High," Mom said, clearing her throat and taking a sip of her wine. Mrs. Prescott took Hampton's non-verbal cue, nodding to my mom and not pressing further. I wondered what exactly she knew; there were many versions of the story that floated around town. I knew from Hampton that Mrs. Prickett already spilled the beans to them both, but I wished I had more details. By the looks of Jane—who stared at her plate with a little crease in the middle of her brows (something she and Hampton shared), she seemed to have lots of questions. The table was quiet. The sounds of scraping forks filled the silence.

"He was in a car accident," I said. "He died."

She nodded, looking apologetic. The crease in her brows remained. I could practically read her thoughts: why would that woman show up here?

I managed a soft smile, cutting into my turkey. My dry mouth coaxed it into tasting like cardboard.

I spoke up, feeling the need to erase the crease on her forehead. "I was there when he died." I paused. "It was an accident, but I hit him with a car."

I felt Annie's sharp gaze on me. Mrs. Prickett murmured something again to Annie, who continued to hold my eye contact.

Mrs. Prescott's lips pressed together. I could practically see the swimming thoughts behind her pupils; *What do I say to something like that?* Or maybe she was thinking, how the hell did she let her son befriend someone like *me*? I shook my head, trying to shake the thought away. I couldn't go there.

"I'm sorry," Jess dropped her fork and knife, clanging

against the plate. She took my dad's champagne glass from my hand, downing the drink. "I need to say something."

"Jess," I said, panicking. "Stop."

She looked at me, shaking her head. "This isn't right. You don't deserve this." I looked at Annie, and her face was ghost-pale. Frozen in time.

"You don't deserve what?" Mom looked between my best friend and me.

"Penny didn't hit Jack with the car." A small gasp came from my mom. My dad was stone. Hampton's hand fell from my knee. I could feel his gaze on me.

"Jess, can I talk to you outside?" Annie asked, rising from her chair. Mrs. Prickett stared at her wine glass, emotionless.

Jess's eyes settled on the school bully. "So you could brainwash me too?"

"What is she talking about?" Dad asked me. My head spun.

"I think it's time we go," Mrs. Prickett finally used her voice, motioning for Annie to join her.

"Annie was driving the car all along. Penny was so freaked out that she... checked out. Annie convinced Penny that she was the one driving, and Penny believed her. Annie told everyone the same story."

"Oh, my God," Mom cried, putting a hand to her mouth. "You didn't do it? How long have you known this?"

"Not long," I whispered, dropping my head to stare at the Thanksgiving napkin in my lap. My fingers grazed the tiny thread of pumpkins, turkeys, and fall leaves.

"What is wrong with you?" Dad asked across the table, his eyes blazing at Annie. "She was your best friend."

"Did you know about this?" Mom craned her neck to look at Mrs. Prickett and, with startling composure, took a breath that raised her shoulders and looked my mom straight in the eyes.

"Yes," she whispered. "I knew." I felt the wind knock out of me, exiting my body and getting as far away from the room as possible.

"I need another drink," Jess mumbled next to me.

Mom let out a cry, covering her mouth again and shaking her head. Mrs. Prescott was rubbing my mom's back, looking nervous, guilty and uncomfortable. I could write a book on all those emotions. *Welcome to Brooks' Thanksgiving: where grieving mothers knock on your door to throw pies, and catastrophic secrets are spilled over the mashed potatoes and turkey.*

Jayden cleared his throat, dropping his fork and wiping his mouth. "Can we have pie now?"

Chapter 27

Jayden's question was ignored; Dad stared at his plate and Mom at Mrs. Prickett, who couldn't seem to take her eyes off her wine glass. I eyed my bare leg, suddenly very aware of the absence of Hampton's hand.

Grandma rose to her feet, her hands firmly on the table for stability. She stared at Annie and her mother, her usually cheerful face robbed by a look of stone. "I think it's time you two leave."

Annie's face was the brightest I'd ever seen; her red-rimmed eyes threatened angry and embarrassed tears. "I'm so sorry," she gushed to my parents, looking between the two of them.

"Annie, don't say another word." Mrs. Pricket ushered fast, crumbling her napkin. Annie looked at her mother like she was seeing her in a whole new light, recognition lighting up her face.

Annie's lips parted. "Mom?" Everyone looked between the two, watching the disaster unravel further and further like a loose ball of yarn.

"I'm so sorry, we were stupid." Annie started.

We?

"Annie, not another word!"

"Sweetie," Grandma said in the most patronizing voice ever, tilting her head at Annie. "I don't think apologies are going to work at this point."

"Don't speak to my daughter like that," Mrs. Prickett said to Grandma, and my mouth dropped. No one ever spoke to Grandma like that. "I think it's time we leave."

"I think that's the best thing you've said all evening," she said. "You're not welcome here." Mrs. Prickett grabbed her daughter's arm, but my mom interrupted their leaving.

"How could you do that to us?" All our attention turned to the principal of Royal High, who met eyes with Mom. A brief guilty look passed her face, but she maintained her composure and put on a fake face, just like she did every day.

"It would've looked worse if the truth came out after everything," she said. "I had my job to think about. Annie's future. It would have caused more pain to everyone." It was silent in the room. Even Jayden didn't make a peep. "The girls are graduating in a few months. What difference does it make? Life moves on."

Jess actually laughed out loud, cracking the still air like a hammer to glass. I attempted to glare at her, but even I couldn't blame her. *Which inspirational poster did she steal that one from?*

"Are you out of your mind?" Mom stood from her seat, her tear-stained cheeks dried and replaced with a new side of anger I'd never seen from her. Like a momma bears anger, protecting her scorned cub.

"Annie, let's go." She turned with her hand on her daughter's shoulder blade, ushering her toward the door. A growing static sound filled my ears. I could feel the over-stimulation in my body, and I resisted the urge to crawl into bed and cover myself with the covers.

Hampton leaned into my ear. "Let's get out here."

I nodded without thinking, the sound of his voice pulling me back to reality. He mentioned the getaway plan to Jess, who nodded and started to join us. Hampton said something to my dad, probably asking if he could take us. Assuming the answer was yes, please, we continued to the front door without any interruption. What I needed most was fresh air. Maybe a visit to the ducks. They always made me feel better. Hampton held onto my hand, the steady pressure suggesting he had no means of dropping it. I started to ask Hampton if we could go there but stopped once the door opened.

Beside me, Hampton turned into a wall. I felt his once-lucid body turn rigid and frozen. Peering at his face, it was a look I'd never seen. It was a mask of twisted surprise and… fear? *Yes, definitely fear*. His nostrils flared, his hand falling from the hold on my hand.

I studied the man; he was a bit taller than my dad, about 6'1", with a thin body and a tattoo that wrapped around his exposed right bicep. An ill-fitting red collared T-shirt hung from his shoulders, clinging to his collarbones. His eyes, brilliantly green, accented a mess of dirty-blond hair, which contrasted against a dark sprinkle of stubble over his chin. Apart from the stubble, he looked shockingly familiar.

"What the hell?" Hampton shifted next to me. I eyed his hands, which balled into fists so tight that his knuckles turned white.

"Hampton!" the man grinned, holding out his arms. "Long-time-no-see." Jess and I exchanged a look, confused.

"Hampton." Mrs. Prescott's voice came from the dining room. It had the same warning tone my dad used moments earlier, but highlighted with—was that anxiety, I heard?

"I came to your house first, but you weren't there, so I asked a neighbor. They said you were celebrating Thanksgiving with friends and then gave me this address."

"Hampton," I murmured, tugging at the sleeve of his shirt.

What was going on?

Slowly, Hampton looked down at me. "It's my dad," he said.
"Your dad?" I repeated.

"His dad," the man—Hampton's dad—said, holding out his arms.

"Give me a hug, kid." Hampton stood still beside me, not crossing the space between them.

"Asher," Mrs. Prescott, appeared beside me, crossing her arms and peeking over her shoulder at the dining room table. Her voice lowered. "What are you doing here?"

"I've come to celebrate Thanksgiving!" Asher grinned. "I thought I'd surprise my family."

"I think you should go," Hampton said firmly.

Asher's smile slipped. "C'mon, Hamp. I thought you'd be more excited to see me."

Jess tugged at my arm, whispering in my ear, "This seems personal. Should we go to your room?" The last place I wanted to be right then was my room.

"Let's take this outside," Mrs. Prescott said, turning to Hampton. "We should go home now. Get your brother."

"You're not inviting me inside?" Asher ignored her, peering past us to look inside the house. "Lincoln's been feeding me crap food for the past six months. The other inmates and I have been dreaming of Thanksgiving mashed potatoes."

Inmates?

"Got any mashed potatoes?"

"Asher, please," she said, sounding urgent at time and moving to join her husband outside. The door clicked shut. Hampton walked into the dining room and leaned down to his brother. I watched him say something to him, with Jayden nodding as his big brother put an arm around his shoulders. Hampton shook my dad's hand, seeming apologetic. By the time he made his rounds with my family, he reached Jess and I at the door.

"I'm really sorry for all of this," he said, avoiding my gaze.

I took his hand, closing the gap between us. "Are you okay?"

Hampton glanced at Jayden, who'd already pulled out his phone and was tapping away. "Yeah, thanks." Yelling started to rise outside the door, and Hampton looked sharply away from me with a hardened gaze.

"I have to go," he said, reaching for the doorknob. "Thank you for inviting us." He didn't wait for my response, and I watched Royal High's celebrity open and shut the door in my face. I'd always assumed Hampton was this perfect New York City hottie whose family moved to a tiny town to get a new start on life. But was I wrong?

Jess joined my side, sipping another glass of champagne she'd poured herself. "What's he hiding?"

Chapter 28

For the next hour, I worked with Jess to clean the kitchen. I ripped a piece of tin foil from its package, simultaneously fitting it over the leftover apple pie and peeking into the dining room. My mom scrubbed the table, particularly Annie and her mother's area. Her teeth were gritted, and the muscles in her bicep popped.

"I'm so happy I ditched my family's Thanksgiving for yours," Jess said. She ripped another piece of tin foil, wrapping a piece of cheese from the appetizer board. "So much more exciting than Uncle Fred playing the same piano song he'd learned when he was twelve." I rolled my eyes, took the cheese from her hand, and unwrapped the tin foil from it. Dad hated when cheese was hidden behind tin foil; he liked to see what exactly his options were. Jess moved to finish up the bottles of champagne, not bothering to get a glass and drinking straight from the bottle.

"You should go over to his house," she said.

"He would think I'm crazy," I said. "Besides, it seems they have some stuff to sort out."

"You got that right." Jess took the last sip of her champagne glass with her right hand, the bottle snug in her left. I tossed some pieces of cheese in the open fridge. "Get in my car. I'm driving you over there." She tossed the empty bottle in the trash, jumping off the counter and swaying a little.

"You just probably drank your weight in champagne," I pointed out, waving a finger at her. "You're not driving."

"Champagne doesn't count." She shooed it away, blinking a little too slowly.

"Where are we going?" Grandma appeared, leaning on the counter and laying her head in her hands.

"Nowhere," I said, while at the same time Jess answered, "Hampton's house."

Grandma straightened, brightening. "I'll drive you right now!" Jess clapped her hands together.

"I have a turkey coma," I lied, feigning a yawn. "I think I'm gonna go lay down for a little."

"Boo!" Jess frowned. "I should get home anyway. Mom'll want me to spend some turkey day with her and the family." She reached out to me for a squeeze; she smelled of champagne.

"Dad," I called into the living room. "Can you drive Jess home?" He glanced up, and I held up the empty champagne bottle for emphasis. Without question, Dad jumped to his feet and swiped his keys from the counter.

When he returned, and by the time the day came to a close and all the leftovers had been officially stored in the fridge, my parents sat me down to debrief all of what they'd learned hours earlier.

"How long have you known this?" Dad asked. Mom sat next to me, quiet.

"Not long."

"Why didn't you tell us?" he asked. "I can't understand how you didn't tell anyone."

"What's it going to change?" I shrugged.

"Sweetie," Mom said, sighing. "So much." I looked at my lap; she was right. For the next hour, we walked through every step of that night. And at the end, something had shifted in the room; it was almost like I was their daughter again. Someone they could recognize. I wasn't sure if it made me feel hurt, or better.

Later, I laid in bed and stared at my ceiling. Regardless of the day's drama, all I could think about was Hampton's hand on my thigh for the majority of the meal. I almost ached to want to be back at that moment. But then I remembered the wounded look on his face when his dad entered the room; I wanted to hug him, comfort him, and let him know that I was there for him if he needed me. I sighed a frustrated sigh, rolling onto my side and watching my reflection in the mirror.

Was I just creating a fantasy in my head? It was just a stupid crush; Hampton wasn't obliged to share his family drama with me.

I clicked the light off near my bed, now staring into the darkness. My eyes took a few moments to adjust, and for a while, I laid there with so many thoughts swarming in my mind: Was Hampton okay? Where, exactly, did his dad come from? How was Jayden doing? His mom? And then, the more selfish thoughts crept in and refused to leave: Did he know how much I liked him? How much do I want him to text me and make plans to hang out? Would he do that soon?

I grabbed my phone from my side table, the harsh light illuminating my face.

Swiping to Hampton's name, I glanced over the few texts between us and typed in the box: *Hope you're doing okay. Want to talk about it?*

I pressed send before I could overthink the wording, not-so-patiently waiting for the bubble to pop up and signal his typing. My heart jumped when it popped up, floated for a second, then disappeared. I frowned, shifting onto my tummy. The bubble never reappeared.

*

I woke up early Monday morning, racing to get ready and paying extra attention to my appearance. Hampton never responded, and I didn't want to look desperate and send a double text (though I contemplated it but was talked down by Jess). The kitchen was quiet as I entered it. I snagged an apple and granola bar, starting toward the garage, before a voice stopped me.

"Good morning!" Grandma chirped. I jumped, startled. She sat nestled in the living room, clutching a cup of tea.

"I didn't see you." I breathed.

"Clearly." She laughed. "What are you in such a hurry for?" The suggestion of something other than school was too obvious to overlook.

The thought of seeing Hampton tugged the corners of my lips upward. "No reason."

"Mhm." She sipped her tea. "Give him my best." I rolled my eyes, saying goodbye and finding Shirley in the garage. Swinging my leg over her, I started my pedal to school. Excitement climbed into my chest as Royal High approached in the distance. I searched the parking lot for his car but didn't see it. I was early, after all. In no time, I parked Shirley and sat on one of the outside benches, scanning the parking lot for the familiar Audi. *Okay, I felt like a bit of a stalker*. But who could blame a girl? Twenty minutes passed, and there was still no sign of him. I shifted, impatient. Of course, he would pick this day to be late.

"Whatcha' doing?" Jess stood next to me, raising an eyebrow.

"Just," I said, pausing, "getting some fresh air."

"Mhm," she said, unconvinced.

"Not waiting for anyone in particular?"

"Just you," I said, linking arms with her. Immediately, we drove into a babble about something stupid her brother did and how her mom grounded him for blah blah blah. I subtly scanned the heads when we reached our lockers, wondering if I'd missed him. First period passed, then the second and third. Still no sign of him. By the time lunch came around, I knew that it was for sure the moment I'd finally track him down. There wasn't a day that went by when he would pass up lunch in the coordinate plane.

But nope, I was wrong. No sign of Hampton Prescott.

"Royal High's celebrity skipping?" Jess questioned me under her breath while in line.

"Weird." My excitement at seeing him was squashed and replaced with worry; first, he didn't respond to my text. And then skip school?

Jess noticed my silence and lightly bumped me. "I'm sure he's fine. Maybe just dealing with his dad." I nodded. I tried to remind myself of that, thinking he just needed a day away from school to decompress, until Tuesday came and went with no sign of Hampton. Then Wednesday, Thursday, and finally, when Friday came and went with still no Hampton, I pedaled hard home with an idea so crazy that I wondered if I were even me any more.

I reached home, and Dad was in the garage working on his car. Grandma's neon green rental car sat parked in the driveway, the sun glinting off the horrid color choice. Apparently, it was the last one available during Thanksgiving weekend, but something told me that Grandma specifically chose the gaudy color.

"Hey, sweet pea," Dad called, glancing over the hood. "How

was school?"

"Good," I said, distracted as I stepped out of Shirley and pushed her to the ground. She landed with a loud thunk, metal hitting pavement, but I didn't even care if her purple and white exterior was scratched.

Not when I had something so preposterous, so out-of-character, and so completely compelling that I had to do it. I stormed inside the house, not bothering to shut the door, and entered the kitchen. Mom and Grandma looked at me, their eyes lingering on my face.

"Are you okay, honey?" Mom asked, pausing in the cutting of vegetables. I'm sure I had a crazy look on my face.

"Grandma?" I ignored her question, directing my attention to her. "Can I borrow your car?" A neighbor was borrowing Mom's car, so I had no other choice. The air in the room stilled; my mom froze, glancing at her mother-in-law as if she were watching a soap opera, waiting for the next line.

Grandma smiled, reaching into her bright purple Chanel purse and retrieving the keys. She handed them to me; the rental keys dangled from her leopard-manicured fingers, crossing the counter and my mom's hands and then falling into mine.

"Give him my best," was all she said, adding a wink and sitting back into her chair.

"Who?" I heard Mom ask, but I was already out the door. Across the driveway, I went, the metal keys dangling from my fingers. Unlocking the door, I slipped into the seat. The car smelled faintly of cigarettes, and I wondered if Grandma snuck out in the night to smoke a few.

I took a breath, eyeing the tree outside my second-floor window. I could feel Dad's eyes on me from the garage, probably just as stunned as my mom was, but I had one objective. I inserted the keys into the ignition, and the rumble of the engine gave me chills.

And I was off.

I'd only been to his house once when I went along for a ride with my mom; she had to drop some casserole things off, some welcome-to-the-town-type-dishes. I drove with memory, and when I'd get nervous or a car passed me on the road, I kept my eyes trained forward and toward the goal at hand: Hampton. Driving Jess's car a few blocks at a time when Port Royal died was a totally different ball game than at rush hour. Or what constitutes rush hour in Port Royal?

On a ride that should have taken me ten minutes but took me twenty, I pulled into his driveway. I parked, feeling suddenly shy. The prior adrenaline had faded, replaced with doubtful thoughts. *Was I being crazy? A stalker? Would he think I was a freak for driving to his house, wondering where he was and why he hadn't been to school in a week?*

I turned off the car, trying to shut out the self-conscious feelings of driving such a crazy-colored car. *Did it make me look even more unhinged?*

I found my feet walking to his door; even my limbs were fed up with my overthinking, and in seconds, I was standing on Hampton Prescott's front doorstep. It was a cute house, painted white with a dark blue trim. The freshly-December air turned the planted shrubbery a faded green, and the cobblestone pathway looked cracked and cold.

I rang the doorbell. Footsteps sounded in the house. The door opened, and Jayden stood there.

"Hi," I said.

Jayden raised an eyebrow. "Hi, Penny."

"Um," I paused. "How are you?"

"Fine," he shrugged. "I just got to a new level in the *Dungeons Dynasty*."

I nodded like I knew exactly what the *Dungeons Dynasty* was.

"That's cool," I said, trying to peer around his shoulder. Some stacked cardboard boxes littered the ground. Maybe Hampton wasn't home. This was a bad idea. My heart hammered against my chest like a drum; *bumbum-bumbum*.

"What are you doing here?" Jayden asked.

"Jayden, who's at the door?" A beautiful, familiar voice filled the silence between us, and suddenly, the door opened wider. There stood Hampton.

His eyes, decorated with slight bags, blinked at me. Once. Twice. Thrice. "Jayden, go help Mom with dinner." Hampton slipped around him, shutting the door.

He crossed his tan arms. All I could do was stare.

"What, uh?" he ran a hand through his hair. "What are you doing here?" My lips parted to answer, but nothing came out. Deja vu hit me like a truck, flashbacking to the day he was on my doorstep.

"I just wanted to make sure you were okay," I said.

He peered around me, eyebrows raising in surprise. "Is that your car?"

"My grandma's," I explained, but I knew that it wasn't what he meant.

"You drove here?" It was a simple question. But at the same time, it wasn't at all.

Yes. I drove there. I, Penny Brooks, operated a vehicle because I *wanted* to.

"Yeah."

I nodded, and in a quick, humiliating turn, something strange happened.

I started to sob. An ugly sob. The kind where you can barely catch your breath and your nose uncontrollably runs, completing the look with aggressive hiccups. You can't even attempt to control it; it is controlling you.

He looked alarmed, like *shit; some girl from school just showed up at my door and started crying*. But Hampton stepped closer, putting his arms around me. One hand found the back of my head as if saying, *I know. I know how hard that was for you.*

"I'm sorry," I croaked. "I didn't mean to—" another croaked sob finished the sentence, and we may have stood there for a few minutes. I was certain his soft, blue shirt was stained with tears and snot. At some point, my hysterics settled into a dainty cry, and he led me to the front step. We sat.

"Are you okay?" he asked, his eyes worriedly searching mine.

I nodded because I was.

"Are *you* okay?" I asked, sniffling. "You haven't been at school all week… and," I paused, "you didn't answer my text."

Hampton hung his head as if expecting this. "I'm sorry I didn't answer. A lot's been going on around here." His expression told me that he was finished talking about whatever it was that'd been "going on."

I nodded, not completely understanding but respecting.

"I'm sorry," I said, swallowing and sniffling, unsure of what else to say. He didn't fill the silence between us. "I guess I came here because…" I stopped.

"No, I *know* I came here to tell you that I like you. And I've been wanting you to know that since you gave me those chips. And honestly, I think I've liked you since I first met you. And I've been wanting to kiss you since our date at the beach, and I went to the bonfire because I wanted to see you, and I'm actually looking forward to going to school again because you're there, and I feel more myself than I did before the accident, and it's because of you." I took a breath, feeling slightly vulnerable that my most-inner feelings were just put out there on the table, available for Hampton to take and embrace or throw away. He looked like I punched him.

Shit. Another one bites the dust, Penny.

I stood, mortified. "I'm sorry, this is probably freaking you out that I showed up here like this."

"No," Hampton interrupted, standing with me and putting a hand around my waist. He dropped it after we met eyes for a moment, looking down and avoiding my gaze.

"What's wrong?" I reached out and touched his jaw, running my thumb over his smooth skin.

"I just wish… you said this earlier."

"I know," I said, relaxing. "I'm sorry. I was just scared and wasn't sure if you liked me like that."

"I get it." Hampton took me into a hug, my head nestling into his broad chest.

Still, he felt tense.

"Is there something wrong?" I asked, pulling away and searching his face.

"I…" Hampton started. "We're moving back to New York." My jaw went slack, and silence filled the sudden gap between us. A silence so stubborn that it refused to be throttled with, but also paired with a precariousness that asked for patience.

"We decided a few days ago," he said. "My dad, um, convinced us to go back with him." My head was spinning with so many questions, but all I felt was devastation for not starting this sooner and for not kissing him when I had the chance.

Hampton's gaze turned stony, and his voice lowered. "He promises he's changed and wants a second chance." I nodded as I understood, but I really had no idea what he was talking about.

"What about school?" I asked.

He nodded like he expected this question. "That's the thing. Mom doesn't want me to move schools again since I'm halfway through the year, and Jayden seems to be doing well."

"So… you're not leaving?" Hope crawled into my chest.

"We are," he said, eyes downcast, "but not until summer." He grabbed my hand, running his thumb across the top. The nerves in my hand tingled. "It's not fair of me to start anything with you when I'll be eventually leaving." *But that was six months from now; couldn't we see what happened?* But even as I thought it, his face wasn't suggesting otherwise.

Something suddenly dawned on me. He was totally just trying to make me feel better. Embarrassed, I started to turn away. "Okay." I nodded. "Well, I guess I'll see you at school." It came out like a question because it's not like we were going to be hanging out or whatever. He had this weird look on his face, as if he'd rather transfer schools than ever see me again, but it was gone in a moment. A long moment. I didn't even wait around to hear his response because it was done. We were done. Even though he and I weren't ever "we," it still felt like something shifted between us.

I walked away from Hampton, back over the walkway and driveway I had walked so confidently over less than fifteen minutes ago. *Boy, can things change?*

I climbed into the green car, somehow more embarrassed by its color than I was when I first arrived. My adrenaline had completely faded, and my actions were operating on a flat line. Hampton had already disappeared, and that's how I knew it was really over.

Chapter 29

I spent the weekend hiding in my room; to say I was mortified to see Hampton again was an understatement.

But as I so cruelly experienced in the past year's events, life goes on.

And that's exactly what I kept telling myself as I passed Shirley that morning, propped upright and waiting for me.

As Mom so casually mentioned over dinner the night before, she didn't need her car the following day, so I was free to take it to school if I didn't feel like riding Shirley.

I took her up on it. Even though things with Hampton took an epic crash and burn, I still made progress in myself. Plus, it was getting colder.

I flicked on my blinker, waiting at a stop light. Despite the lingering humiliation that was staring me in the face, I was proud of myself for taking a step—no, a leap—forward in life. I pulled into the school, parking away from other cars. I couldn't stay rooted in the past any more. I had to keep moving.

Just like that first day of school months prior, I ducked my head and prayed I wouldn't see Hampton. Or he wouldn't see me. I mean, why wasn't I talked down to? Why didn't someone say, "Hey, Penny, maybe don't drive to Hampton's house unannounced and practically beg to be together?" I shook my head to somehow shake the thought away, pulling open the school doors.

As I made my way to my locker, running through all the

ways I would avoid seeing you-know-who, I stopped in my tracks, my eyes falling on her.

Annie stood ramrod straight in front of Jack's memorial, her face utterly blank and pale. But I knew better; it was pain. For the first time ever, I saw how she felt. I saw her mourning her boyfriend's death, not my own mistakes, her mistakes, or even Jack's mistakes.

"Annie?" It came out of my mouth before I had time to think, and my feet stepped closer without permission. She looked at me, and for the first time in a long time, it didn't look like she hated me.

I joined her without another word, and together, we looked at the numerous portraits, personalized awards, and group photos with Jack, almost as if we were waiting for something to happen, for him to come around the corner, laughing about something that happened that weekend or in soccer practice. But the same chatter of surrounding students bounced around us, and we stood quiet in the midst of it all.

"It was my fault," she said. "All my fault." I found myself shaking my head. The bell rang for class, but neither of us moved.

She turned to me, anger flashing in her hazel eyes. They were lighter in color that day, reflecting off her white shirt. "I'm the one who forced you to drive. I'm the one who made Jack come in the car with us and who was such a bitch to you that I didn't even notice him get out." I don't know what made me do it, but I wrapped my arms around her shaking shoulders. Her tears fell faster than her racing heartbeat. "I'm the reason we're not friends any more. I'm the reason he's dead." Her last sentence hung in the air, suffocating the molecules around us.

I sucked in a breath, holding her. "It's *all* our fault. I'm just as much to blame as you are." I paused. "And so is Jack." She pulled away from me, her eyes dripping with tears. By that point, we were alone in the hallway. Class was underway.

I folded my arms, then unfolded them. "I think…" I searched for the right words. "I think I was so caught up in my own grief that I didn't think about anyone else. I didn't think about what you were going through, or what his friends were going through, or literally anyone else who knew him."

"It's not like I let you," she said in a tiny voice, sniffling. "I—"

"Sweetie? Are you okay? Why aren't you in class?" Mrs. Prickett exited her office with a softened look on her face that turned hard when she saw me. Glancing between both her daughter and I, she drew a conclusion.

"What did you do?" the principal asked me, waving a finger in my face. I swallowed hard, stepping back.

"Penelope, I've had it. You've caused so much distress in Royal High that I think it's time we—"

"Mom," Annie stopped her mother. She wiped the tears off her face, her shoulders rising from the breath she took and held. "Stop."

"Annie, this girl—" she started with a voice that trembled slightly, but my ex-best friend finished with, "did nothing. You've known that this whole time."

Finally, everything fell into place. It was all a game, and Mrs. Prickett was the instigator of it all.

My lips parted in shock; no sound came out. "You told her to do it, didn't you?" I watched Mrs. Prickett's face tense, refusing to surrender the act she'd so beautifully crafted since the night of Jack's death.

Annie looked to the ground, but Mrs. Prickett held her stance and stared back at me. "I don't know where you got that from, Penelope, but it's—"

"Yes," Annie said, swallowing hard and looking at me. "She told me to do it. To tell everyone that it was you and to keep the act going."

I imagined Annie calling her mother on the phone, crying, explaining what happened, earning a response of, "Annie, calm down. I want you to make Penny believe she did it. Can you do that?"

"Annie, get to class," Mrs. Prickett said. But no one moved.

"I can't believe you did that to me," I said to her, a mother, an adult, the principal of my high school, the woman who watched me grow up. "How could you?" I felt pressure swirling around me, pressing into my chest.

Mrs. Prickett blinked, her eyes welling with tears. "I had to do what was best for my daughter." I turned away from them both, my bag bouncing on my hip as I stormed down the hallway, tears blurring my vision as I rounded the corner and slammed into a hard body.

*

"Penny?" I looked up at Hampton, and *I swear*, did the universe hate me? "Are you okay?" He searched my face, putting a hand on my cheek, and, as if remembering our last conversation, took it away.

Maybe it was the fact that Annie's mother planted this whole story about me and was the sole proprietor of the shitty life I lived for the last four months.

Maybe it was the tears that were dropping from my eyes, obscuring the stupid high school halls that I so desperately wanted to leave and graduate from in less than six months.

Or maybe it was the fact that I just didn't give a shit any more, that life was short, and you're never going to get what you want out of this life if you just sit back. And not kiss the boy in front of you.

And that's exactly what I did.

"Penny?" he said again, and I answered by filling the gap between us and pressing my lips firmly to his. My stomach did this little lurch, as if demanding an answer to whatever the hell I was doing. His lips, startled against mine, softened, and kissed me back. They were soft and warm, just as I expected them to be, at all the times I imagined kissing them. His arm found my waist, pulling me closer to him and flush against his chest. I tightened my grip on the back of his neck, deepening the kiss, and then pulled away.

He looked at me like he wanted to kiss me again. "What was that?" he whispered, his warm breath fanning my face. It smelled of spearmint gum and a touch of blue Gatorade.

I sighed, touching my forehead to his. "I've had a really bad day."

"What are you like on a good day?"

I couldn't help but let out a short laugh. "Do you want to go somewhere with me?" Yes, I was aware it was eight in the morning on an active school day. But I didn't care, and judging by his face, he didn't care either. With a nod, I led him out the double doors I'd entered less than twenty minutes ago.

*

I brought him to a place I hadn't visited in a while, and it looked like my duckling friends had found a new place. The usual ripple of the water was calm, disturbed only by the occasional breeze and gentle current.

"Secluded spot," Hampton said, looking around. He sat on the sand. "Is this where you tell me your darkest secrets?" It was the only place I didn't have to think about Mrs. Prickett and her betrayal. I didn't go there to tell him that she was the instigator. I went there to get away for just a moment.

I shook my head, joining him on the sand. "Pretty sure you know all of mine."

"Well, I have one," he said, and I looked at him, waiting. "I didn't want to tell you that day because you were just so excited, but I'm actually allergic to chocolate." I stared. And in seconds, I burst into laughter.

"And potato chips," he said, scrunching his nose. "And carrots." *God, he was cute.*

Come to think of it, I remembered his little coughs and brief moments of pause before eating. "Why didn't you tell me, you weirdo?"

"I didn't want to hurt your feelings." He shrugged, grinning and looking out toward the little opening.

"Well, was it good?" I asked.

"Was it *good*?" He repeated, mock-gasping and holding a hand to his heart. "I ate something I'm allergic to, and you're wondering if I enjoyed myself?"

"Okay, okay," I said, surrendering. "Were you okay?"

"My legs went numb by the time we got to the car, but I had my epi-pen—" I hit him on the shoulder, his *oh-so-strong* shoulder, before he finished it with laughs of his own. "Yes, I was fine. I didn't eat enough to paralyze me."

"Stop it!"

We fell into an easy silence; a breeze blew, the sound of the seagrass brushing together and playing as background music to our little moment.

"So, real talk?" He finally broke the silence, his tone soft.

"Why did you bring me here?"

I found myself shaking my head, blinking at the grainy sand between my toes. "This is where I came to get a break from being me." He was quiet, giving me space to continue. "I would tell my parents I was going to a friend's or doing something social, but really, I came here with a ziploc bag of bread to feed the ducks." My cheeks reddened. *I can't believe I just said that.*

"I used to feed ducks with my dad," he said, sounding reminiscent. "Before… everything." A look passed his face, but it was gone in an instant, and he continued, "It was fun. Therapeutic."

I nodded along, and he turned to me with a grin. "So, what you're saying is that I should feel special for being brought to your hiding spot?"

I hid a smile. "Oh, I bring guys here all the time." His grin slipped just a tad before I rushed to fix what I'd done. "I'm kidding." He didn't seem too convinced, but I decided I'd let it stay that way. For now, at least. There was something I'd been wondering since it happened. "Who told you Justin and I were together?"

Someone had to have spun up the lie and let it loose. "No one." His eyes flickered to mine for just a moment. "I actually saw you guys one day. Outside the coordinate plane." Of course, when we were spilling our guts and hugging and nearly kissing… who could blame anyone for thinking we were together. I shook my head. "I should have been more careful. That was just… it was a goodbye." It was more than that, of course, but it was the wholehearted truth: Justin and I were addressing a much-needed closure to our puppy-love relationship.

He scooted closer to me. "Let's talk about that kiss." My lips parted, my eyes darting to his lips for just a moment before I looked quickly away.

"Sorry, I—"

He put a hand on my arm to stop me. "I'm happy one of us had the balls to do it."

I smiled, my chest and tummy feeling warm. *So, Jess was right.*

"I'm the one who should be apologizing," he started, eyes so clear and wide and trained on me that I almost had to look away. "I figured how big of a deal it was to get in a car and drive to my house to tell me how you feel. I should have done the same, then and there. I try every day to be a little better of a person, and I… totally failed that day." I remembered to take a breath, my heart sounding loud in my ears.

"Do you think…" He paused, shy. "Do you think we could try this again? I promise I'll try to be better."

"Me too," I said. I'd made so much progress already, and I knew that with every passing day, I would be a better version of myself with Hampton for as long as we had together, even if that was just until summer.

"So, is that a yes?" I don't remember how it happened, but he was inches from my face, waiting for an answer. I smiled, leaning in, and just when my lips about brushed his, a loud *quack!* sound filled in the would-be kiss. Our heads craned to the water, and one—just one—duck floated into the opening. A brown spot accented the side of its face, and instantly, I knew.

"It's Penny!" I practically yelled in his face. He was startled. "What?"

"The duck! I named her Penny." I explained, looking

excitedly at my pal. Hampton looked at her. "You named a duck… after yourself?"

"Only because she was always by herself instead of with the rest of her siblings, so I resonated with her." I paused, ducking my head. "That actually sounds more depressing out loud, now that I say it."

"Just a little." He chuckled, tilting his head at the duck floating peacefully in the water, neck high. Probably waiting for food from me. She was a little bigger than the last time I saw her.

"She's independent," Hampton said after we watched her for a bit, looking at me. His voice grew softer. "I like that." We watched Penny until she swam away and out the opening, then chatted about school, teachers, and some rumor that Eric had been held back four times from graduating. Hampton believed it; I semi-believed it.

"So I actually have another secret," he said.

I wrinkled my nose. "You don't have good secrets. Remember the first one you ever told me?"

Hampton screwed his lips together. "So, I lied. I actually do like beer."

"So, you're a liar too?" I laughed.

"Well, I promised you I would tell you a better one at some point," he said. He leaned into my ear before waiting for a response. Slowly, his breath tickled my ear as he whispered, "I think I could fall in love with you. Fast." He drew away, our faces inches apart, and we kissed. He threw a tentative arm around my waist, then, after a moment, tightened his grip and pulled me closer. This kiss differed from the one in the hallway of Port Royal High; this kiss bled notes of contentment, mutual understanding, and a passionate, lingering taste of something to look forward to.

I wasn't sure how long it went on for, but it was suddenly cut short with the shrill ring of a phone. We broke apart, looking at each other and taking a shy breath. It was my phone, and I scrambled for it in my backpack before finding it.

"Jess?" I asked. Hampton dragged a finger alongside my forearm. Most of my attention was diverted to him, his touch, and the way he was making my whole body feel with just one finger.

"Penny," she said, her voice sounding low and urgent. "Where are you?"

"Um, with Hampton," I said. His finger led a trail to my collarbone, another finger joining. Chills erupted over my skin. *God, Jess, whatever this was, it better be good.*

I ignored the pause on the other end, knowing we'd revisit the fact that I was with a favorite senior. "The whole school." She stopped, and the phone fumbled like she was moving. Her voice lowered. "The school is going crazy looking for you."

"And Hampton?" Geez, kids skipped classes all the time. And we were seniors.

What was the big deal?

"No, just you. Principal Prickett announced your name, like, five times, over the speaker," she said.

Huh?

Her voice sounded like she was underwater. "Where are you? You sound weird."

"The bathroom," she said. "Only place I could think of to be alone during my class. But, um, Penny..." I didn't like the newfound trepidation in her voice.

"What?" Hampton fingers continued to blaze a trail over my skin, now entangling themselves in my hair.

"What happened this morning with you and Mrs. Prickett? And Annie?" My head hitched back a bit. He pulled his hand back. I'd run out with Hampton right after our blowout; there was no way I'd told Jess yet. How did she know about that? "What do you mean?"

"Well," I heard the shutting of the bathroom door. I imagined her closing herself in and leaning against the wall. "People are talking. They're saying how you had some sort of psychotic break, or something, in the hallway this morning. How you were accusing Mrs. Prickett of, um, lying about Jack's death to everyone? And how Annie went along with it—"

"But, Jess—" I started, but she cut me off.

"I know, I know. It's true. But it sounds crazy to someone who doesn't truly know the she-devils." I tried to rack my brain for why she would be causing such a scene, and then it clicked: **Mrs. Prickett was scared. She was worried** I went off and told everyone the truth, and now she was trying to make it seem like I was the crazy one.

I had a bad feeling in my tummy. I shifted on the sand. I so wanted him to continue touching me, but I felt too sick to even let myself be distracted by his touch. "What do you mean, 'people are talking'?"

She was quiet for a moment. "I mean, they had to cancel some classes because people were so worked up over the drama."

"I..." I started, not able to say anything else. My face reddened. A little from embarrassment. But mostly from anger. *When was I going to catch a break?*

"Um, Penny," she said. Her voice sounds clearer, like she'd come up for air. I rubbed my temples.

"What?"

"The cops are here. Parked outside. They must've just gotten here."

"Oh, my god." I rubbed my temples, imagining Mrs.

Prickett's frantic phone call: *nine-one-one? Yes, I'm calling about a disturbed student who's throwing tantrums in my hallways. She's taken off, and I'm scared of what she might do.*

"You should get here." I was already off the sand and headed back, with Hampton trailing behind me with no clue as to what was going on.

"What's happening?" Hampton asked, climbing into the car. He started it.

I buckled my seatbelt. "Mrs. Prickett." He just nodded. He was about to see it all go down. We got to the school in minutes; Jess was right. Two cop cars were messily parked in the handicapped spots.

"Whoa," Hampton murmured, looking at me. "Starting to think I should've asked for more information." But I couldn't really hear him; I was too angry. He parked. I climbed out, heading toward the entrance and half-expecting to be tackled to the ground. If only I knew what Mrs. Prickett said about me.

With Hampton behind me, I opened the doors and found myself to be the center of attention. Lingering students stood by the row of lockers, eyes locked on me as I walked toward Principal Pickett's office.

Shoulders back, head high.

I could do this.

The lady herself spotted me through the glass window to her office; she pointed over the officer's shoulders, right at me.

I couldn't do this.

I stopped. Hampton's hard chest ran into my back. A crowd was forming. I spotted Justin.

"Penny?" one of the officers said slowly, as if detonating a bomb. He and his partner took slow, calculated steps toward me like they were walking through sand. My heart hammered in my chest, tricking my nerves into wanting to cut and run like I was actually the psychotic girl who made up a terrible lie. Just when I felt my feet stepping back, Jess reached my side. She grabbed my wrist, squeezing to let me know I wasn't alone. If it were even possible, Hampton stepped closer to me. His hand grazed the low of my back. I could do this.

"Penny, sweetheart," Principal Prickett said. "I've called your therapist, Dr. Yao, and she's on the way." Some snickering sounded from my audience. My face reddened.

Royal High's Queen Bee stood off to the side, adding to the crowd of watchful gazes. But hers was different; *she* was the one who looked embarrassed, avoiding the show the student body found themselves engrossed in.

The principal lowered her voice, acting every bit of the part of an adult who treats students respectfully and fairly. "I called the police because of the incident this morning. And how you went on about me covering up Mr. Doe's"—she sniffled—"death."

"Penelope," the other officer said.

"Her name is Penny," Hampton interjected.

"Penny. Are you feeling better?"

"As opposed to what?" I asked.

"This morning. Principal Prickett has been very worried for you," he said.

"Psycho," someone coughed. The students laughed.

"Students," Prickett scolded.

"So, let me get this straight." Aaron stepped forward from the growing crowd, seeming a bit pissed and looking straight at me. "You can't deal with the fact that you killed Jack, so you're blaming it on our principal? What is wrong with you, Penny?" Some exclamatory remarks came from the crowd, including curse words and derogatory commentary on my "precarious" mental health.

And then, Aaron said something that silenced the crowd. "You should've died in that crash instead of him." I looked at him, the boy who I'd known since we were little kids, and felt like I'd been punched.

"You're sick, Aaron," Jess said.

"I'm the sick one?" He jabbed a finger at his chest. "How about the girl standing next to you who still can't seem to accept the responsibilities of her actions?"

"She's more than taken responsibility, Aaron," Hampton said. "Don't be a dick."

"Oh, and you've been here all of, what?" He counted his fingers. "Five minutes? You don't know shit, Prescott."

"I know more than you, asshole." Hampton stepped in front of me, taking bounding strides toward Aaron. He pushed him; Aaron slammed into the locker, and I don't know who threw the first punch, but a fight broke out in a tangle of arms and fists. The cops, realizing that this wasn't a movie, jumped to attention to break up the two boys.

Until something happened that shook the hallways of Royal High so badly that it still hasn't recovered.

"Stop! Stop!" Annie screamed, jumping into the jumble of police uniforms and teenage boys. Once the long blonde hair intercepted the punches and cursing and pushing, the hallway fell quiet, waiting for Annie's next move.

As usual, everyone's eyes were set on her. Annie looked at her mom, her shoulders drooping. "I can't do this any more."

"Annie, come to my office right now." Principal Prickett ushered her daughter, but for once, she stood her ground and shook her head.

"I did it," Annie announced. "I'm the one who was driving the car that hit Jack."

"What?" one of her friends blurted.

Annie's chin trembled. "I told everyone it was Penny's fault. I made it up. And my mother went along with it." The gazes of my peers found me, but it felt different. Softer. Relief washed over me, all the way from the top of my head to my feet. My head felt light.

"You're telling the truth?" the officers beside her asked.

She nodded. "The whole truth." I didn't know much about criminal offenses, but I knew lying to the police was definitely one. The hallway fell silent.